The Hidden Empire

by

Thomas Velsun

The Hidden Empire

COPYRIGHT © 2024 by Henry Thomas Jones III

Contact Information: info@thewildrosepress.com

Cover Art by *Lea Schizas*

The Wild Rose Press, Inc.
PO Box 708
Adams Basin, NY 14410-0708
Visit us at www.thewildrosepress.com

Publishing History
First Edition, 2024
Trade Paperback ISBN 978-1-5092-5835-2
Digital ISBN 978-1-5092-5836-9

Published in the United States of America

Chapter 1

In Jacksonville, Florida, Ralph Gibson, President of Tuxtun Industries (Tuxtun) and Matt Baker, Vice President of Tuxtun, sat at the round conference table in Ralph's office with Ben Fulton, Special Agent in Charge (SAC) of the Jacksonville FBI Office.

From Ben's expression, Matt knew some bad news was coming.

"Well, we chased Hugo Wagner out of the United States, but we haven't gotten rid of him," Ben said. "According to the latest intelligence report I've received, his main goal right now is to kill both of you as soon as possible. With his super-advanced technology, he's a huge danger to all of us. He's a madman who must be eliminated."

Matt leaned forward. "I thought his goal was to conquer the world."

Ralph nodded.

"That's for later," Ben said. "It looks like he holds a big grudge, and his main concern is removing you and everyone around you from his path."

"Is Hugo still in Germany?" Ralph asked.

"Yes, the CIA has just verified that, but they aren't sure of his specific location. They think he's in northern Germany in the Hartz Mountains and has a fortress that's equipped with futuristic capability," Ben said. "He can stay in his fortress and orchestrate different types of attacks on multiple locations around the world."

Matt narrowed his eyes and waited for Ben to continue.

"Based on the latest intelligence I've received, I think we're going to be hearing from Hugo one way or another real soon," Ben said. "I wanted to come over and warn you. I also wanted to give you some new information."

"Isn't Germany, the German Military in particular, taking full responsibility for capturing him and bringing him to justice?" Matt asked.

Ben nodded. "Intelligence analysts in our Washington office have advised me the German Military is launching their first initiative tomorrow morning." He stared at Matt and Ralph. "If they don't eliminate Hugo, I'm sure we're still going to be involved in some aspects of this. That's a big reason I wanted to come over and discuss some things with you face to face."

Matt slowly rubbed his chin. He appreciated the heads-up from Ben but hoped he and Ralph could soon get back to concentrating full-time on running the Tuxtun business.

Ben leaned forward. "Thanks again to both of you for your help in driving Hugo Wagner out of the country. However, because he's now in Germany doesn't mean we can forget about him. We still have some work left. We've done a good job snuffing out Hugo's former operations here in the United States, but our profile on him shows he holds grudges and he's probably going to stay extremely vindictive for our doing that." Ben's sober gaze again took in both Matt and Ralph. "The two of you proved to be the most trouble for him. Based on his profile, he's not going to rest until he kills both of you."

Ralph grunted. "That's nothing new for us."

Matt nodded. "We're both in top form to protect ourselves and we plan to stay that way."

"Good. You both still look more like professional athletes than you do business executives. I guess you're continuing all of your weight-lifting exercises and such?" Ben gave the two men a quizzical glance.

"Yes, and on a regular basis," Matt said.

Ralph gestured toward Matt. "He's still a little better than I am on most things. I bench press a little over three hundred pounds, but he stays about thirty pounds ahead of me."

"Staying in top physical shape will continue to be a great asset," Ben said. "It looks like we'll again have some big challenges coming up right here at home. That's another thing I wanted to come over and talk about." He narrowed his eyes. "Elements of the World Bank, the International Monetary Fund (IMF), and the World Trade Organization (WTO) have again established some type of joint office here in the Jacksonville area. There's no direct information about who funds this office, but our financial analysts in the FBI tell me none of the money comes directly from any part of the World Bank, the IMF, or the WTO. It looks like Hugo could be back to his old tricks."

Matt shrugged. "We're already aware Hugo has set up a lot of dummy corporations that move money around through a lot of the global monetary institutions to make funding their various projects as invisible as possible."

"Yeah, and it's time to take another look at all that," Ben said. "I'll set up a meeting at our FBI headquarters here in Jacksonville to discuss that in more detail real soon."

Ralph leaned forward. "I'll get my executive team together right after you leave and bring them up to date. We'll review all the aspects of the situation and be prepared to move forward quickly."

Ben gave a thumbs-up and stood.

Matt and Ralph walked with Ben toward the front entrance.

"Let's hope the German Military has some success tomorrow," Ben said. "If they can eliminate the threat Hugo Wagner poses, it will be a huge relief. I'll keep you posted."

Chapter 2

The sun hovered in a clear blue sky on this early September morning in northern Germany.

Everything was peaceful and serene around the countryside until the loud thunder from three Euro-Copter Tiger helicopters rumbled through the foothills of the Hartz Mountains.

Since Hugo Wagner was now an internationally known criminal and rumored to have his new headquarters at a secluded mountainous location in northern Germany, the German Government partnered with the United States Government to try to locate him.

The German President, German Military, and German law enforcement were fully cooperating with their counterparts in the United States.

After receiving a tip last week about Hugo Wagner having a high-tech fortress in the Hartz Mountains, the German Military deployed a detail of helicopters to find it and pinpoint its location.

The pilot on the left flank of the formation pushed a button on his tactical microphone. "I've been scanning the area below us. Nothing stands out. Does anyone have any new thoughts on how to spot our target?"

The pilot in the lead helicopter replied, "We were told to look for an unusual structure, something like a fortress. I don't have anything new to add."

The pilot on the right flank said, "I don't have any new thoughts either, and you're right about nothing standing out down there."

As the three helicopters approached the eastern part of the search area, the leader continued scanning the area below him. "Keep your formation and keep looking."

When the three helicopters got into the foothills and closer to the mountains, the leader said, "Let's slow down to fifty miles an hour, drop our altitude to three hundred feet, and circle the area a few times before we move to the higher ground. If we don't spot anything unusual within the next thirty minutes, we'll turn south and head back to base. Follow me and keep scanning the area carefully."

The leader slowed, reduced his altitude to three hundred feet, and banked to his left.

The other two pilots followed in perfect formation.

"Stay alert and look for anything unusual on the ground, moving or otherwise," the leader said.

A brief silence ensued as the three helicopters continued their turn at fifty miles per hour.

"I see something unusual down there, real unusual," the pilot on the right flank said.

The leader glanced out at the landscape toward his right. "What do you see?"

"Some odd-looking trucks, three of them. They just emerged from under a group of trees. They're moving in our direction."

"Turn south immediately. Go as fast and as high as you can as quickly as possible!" the leader exclaimed. "Those trucks could be mobile missile-launchers."

After completing a quick turn to the south, the

three helicopters shot forward at high speed.

They sped up rapidly and ascended quickly.

Urgently scanning the area, the leader got a glimpse of three smoke trails coming toward them.

In another second, each of the three helicopters exploded.

Three fireballs crashed to the ground.

Chapter 3

At eleven a.m. local time in a mountainous region in southern Germany, Hugo Wagner, Oleg Titov, and Wan Lu sat at a doughnut-shaped round table positioned in the middle of their hi-tech control room.

The opening in the middle of the round table measured twenty feet in diameter and contained four hi-tech chairs that could rotate in a full circle. Hugo, Oleg, and Wan occupied three of them.

Hugo was short and chubby and had a strong urge to control everything he could. He knew Napoleon and Hitler had been short too and they obviously had the same urge. However, they hadn't seemed to be as smart as he was. They hadn't taken the time to plan every detail from beginning to end. They had been too impatient—he wasn't.

Hugo glanced at his partners.

Oleg was about six feet tall with a stocky build. He had classical Russian features.

Wan was about the same height as Oleg, but he was very slim. His coloring and slanted eyes reflected his Chinese heritage.

All three men were highly intelligent and capable of accomplishing difficult tasks. That's why they were billionaires.

Hugo smiled inwardly. In spite of their recent failure in the United States, they were a good team. And they all committed themselves to their common goal of conquering the world.

The control room was round, about fifty feet in diameter, and had a curved computer screen that fit the contour of the room. The large screen extended from floor to ceiling all the way around the room.

The table had a circular desktop extending two feet out from the doughnut hole in the center. A small section of the desktop could be lifted to allow people into the center area.

After rotating his chair a few degrees, Hugo glanced at Oleg and Wan. "Well, our first mission conceived at this location has just succeeded."

The three men laughed.

"It was a brilliant plan indeed to put some missile launchers in the Hartz Mountains," Oleg said. "They'll still think we're somewhere in that area in northern Germany and they'll concentrate their attention up there."

All three men continued to laugh.

"Okay, let's get to the next item of business," Hugo said. He rotated his chair a few more degrees and placed the red dot from his laser pointer on an image showing the site of the Tuxtun headquarters building in Jacksonville, Florida. "Our satellites are in place all over the world and all of our other spying equipment is fully functional. The trillion dollars I spent on this setup was well worth it."

Wan nodded. "We have over ten thousand programs running at the same time on the quantum computer. We have a super high-speed internet and each program searches for specific things we want to know, and displays related images and information instantly. We have the best artificial intelligence on the planet."

Oleg grunted. "Yeah, and the parts for the security system we installed at this location are the best money can buy. Our combined engineering group applied their skills and here we are with the best AI and the best security on the planet." He extended his hands to his side with his palms up.

Hugo gestured toward the image highlighted by the red dot. "We have some of our most advanced spy satellites trained on the Tuxtun headquarters and we're monitoring and recording all of their phone calls. We have the very best of German, Russian, and Chinese engineering. With our intelligence gathering and hi-tech capability, we'll be impossible to stop."

He made a fist with his right hand and raised it high into the air. "We'll eliminate Baker and Gibson and then we'll continue our activity to conquer the world. We'll conquer the United States first and move on quickly from there."

Oleg and Wan each gave a thumbs-up.

Hugo scanned the multiple displays. "The programming for the quantum computer seems to be working to perfection. We have a ton of information about a lot of things that concern us." He focused his laser pointer on another one of the multiple displays which collectively covered all the space on the circular wall. "That information in particular."

Both Oleg and Wan studied the information around the area of the red dot while they waited for Hugo to continue.

"Our system is in place where all the individuals on our teams of analysts work in shifts to constantly monitor the information and immediately report on anything urgent," Hugo said. "In addition to our teams of analysts we use as backup, we also have handheld devices programmed with our best artificial intelligence to give us alerts. We can monitor everything going on without having to be here in the control room."

Wan grunted. "And every capability we have is backed up by another system. That's the smart way to operate."

"Since Jake Bolton delivered the warning from the so-called Hidden Empire, do you still have him in place to advise us?" Oleg asked.

"Of course," Hugo said. "He's staying alert for any clues to the identities of any individuals in the secret group who contacted him earlier."

Wan nodded. "With our capability, we should be able to discover any hidden organization out there if one actually exists."

"Maybe this has some connection to that," Hugo said as he again focused his gaze on the information around the red dot from his laser pointer. "The International Acceptance Bank of New York had a record number of transactions this last week."

"Why is that significant?" Oleg asked.

"That bank was founded in 1921 by one of the founders of the Federal Reserve System," Hugo said. "He apparently felt the need to establish another legitimate internationally known institution to enhance the global money flow he could use for his purposes, mainly getting more money."

Oleg narrowed his eyes and looked directly at Hugo. "Can you be more specific?"

"I understand the general aspects but I can't

explain all the specific details," Hugo said. He looked at Wan. "Maybe you can do that. You have the most financial knowledge among the three of us."

Wan gave a slight shrug. "It's likely this secret group we referenced uses this bank for their purposes, and the details are far too complicated to explain simply. Acceptance banking is basically a process of guaranteeing repayments of loans. Let's just say this additional process in the global money flow further legitimizes things and helps move large amounts of money to the intended destinations. It also generates a lot of additional income for its owners by charging fees for its services."

Both Hugo and Oleg nodded slowly and didn't comment.

"As more time passed, the powers behind the global money flow decided they also needed the World Bank, the IMF, and the WTO," Wan said. "These institutions were added to the global monetary system much later on."

Hugo stared at the men before him. "Now let's get back to thinking about why the International Acceptance Bank of New York has just had a huge increase in transactions." He glanced at Wan. "Go ahead and have your experts check into the situation. That way we don't have to spend a lot of time trying to determine the reasons for the surge."

Wan nodded. "I'll have some of my best financial experts in China look into this and report their findings back to me."

"Good," Hugo said. "Let's decide what our next move should be for moving us forward in our quest to dominate the world."

Each man raised his right fist high in the air.

Chapter 4

Later that day in Jacksonville, Matt Baker and Ralph Gibson sat at the large table in the main conference room at Tuxtun with six other people.

Three of them at the table were also from Tuxtun: Judy Caldwell (business analyst), Todd Green (technology specialist), and Steve Baxter (security chief).

Justin Mason, the Jacksonville Police Chief, Vince Simmons, the Saint Augustine Police Chief, and Ben Fulton completed the group at the table.

"Well, I just got some bad news right before I left to come over here," Ben said. "The German Military failed to locate Hugo Wagner's hideout and all three search helicopters were shot down."

"Are they going to continue their efforts?" Ralph asked.

"That's my understanding, but they expect the United States to start providing some support," Ben said. "And, of course, some of that got delegated down to us. We've had a lot of experience dealing with Hugo, and there could be some related activity over here that needs attention." He scanned the faces around the table. "Obviously, the CIA and the Military will need to take the lead on all the international aspects of this but I think our local effort will still be needed. I hope everyone here will agree to continue working on this, especially concerning the headquarters of this new global financial operation being established in our area."

Ralph gave a slow nod and looked at Judy. "We've discussed this and you're our financial expert. Any thoughts?"

"I'm a firm believer in following the money," Judy said. "It now looks like much of the funding for this new global financial office in the Jacksonville area is funneled through shell corporations. That's characteristic of Hugo Wagner being involved. Multiple new accounts have been established on the Isle of Man and the Channel Islands. Todd and I will continue our research. The process is complex. They obviously want to keep the real sources of the funding hidden."

Todd leaned forward. "And we might be dealing with a lot more than Hugo Wagner and his group this time. There's definitely another layer of global transactions above those we've traced to Hugo's organization. Judy and I have discovered there's a very secretive global group of power-elites who are directly involved in the money flow, calling themselves the Hidden Empire. They essentially control the major economic activities in the world. We might be dealing with them too before we finish investigating this new office."

Matt nodded. "Whoever is involved in the operations of this office isn't going to like our investigating their activity." He looked at Judy. "Do you have any idea why someone felt a need to establish this office over here?"

"Since Hugo Wagner set up a similar one before, it's probably for the same reasons," Judy said. "Todd and I have uncovered some clues about the details. We'll both work hard to find all the answers."

"I had the same question about why someone would want to establish this office over here and I asked our financial analysts at the FBI to get some answers," Ben said. "Our analysts concluded various aspects of all the global monetary organizations are used by some powerful groups to secretly funnel money to activities and organizations they want to support. Hugo's group is one of them, but not the only one. Having an office in the United States with specialists from each of the global organizations makes things easier in a lot of ways."

"Do you think one of the powerful groups you mentioned is the Hidden Empire?" Judy asked.

Ben narrowed his eyes. "Many of our financial analysts in Washington think so. You and Todd need to start working closely with them. This is something we need to gain more insight into."

Judy glanced at Ralph.

Ralph gave a thumbs-up.

Matt looked at Judy. "I know you don't like to speculate, but you mentioned you and Todd had some clues about some of the details. Would you make some guesses?"

"Our Federal Reserve is also part of the overall global money flow and the people who established the office here probably intend to have a lot of face-to-face meetings to avoid their phone calls being intercepted by the National Security Agency," Judy said. "Having an office over here in the United States makes things a lot easier."

Matt nodded. "That makes sense. We know NSA

has improved their technology. Phone calls can now be intercepted no matter how good their encryption is."

"Right," Judy said. "Hugo, in particular, wants to reduce the number of phone calls."

Ben leaned forward. "This new global financial office is south of Jacksonville, close to Saint Augustine. Some of us need to visit and ask a few questions. We might find out we have more to be concerned about than we're aware of at the moment."

Ralph nodded. "If Judy's right and any aspects of this new office prove to be directly connected to Hugo Wagner, this could get very complicated for us."

"We can be certain Hugo and his partners have their quantum computer functioning in their new stronghold in Germany," Matt said. "They have enough money to afford a super technological setup with the best artificial intelligence, spy satellites, and such. This situation will probably continue to get more complex and more difficult to untangle."

Todd narrowed his eyes. "We know a lot of groups are involved in the total conspiracy. Too bad one of them is our Federal Reserve. The owners of the Federal Reserve have always been masters of disguise as it applies to what they're really doing. They have a long history of covering things up."

"We already know a lot about what you're probably going to say, so don't bother giving us a history lesson," Ralph said.

Todd flashed a ghost of a smile and then shrugged. "Just wanted to remind everyone about the depth of what we're dealing with."

"Except for the Hidden Empire, I think we're all well aware of whom we're dealing with," Ralph said.

"Many people connected directly to the Federal Reserve have been ruthless about things over the years, and they're probably still that way. Many descendants of the founders are still in place."

Matt grunted. "Yeah, and if they're directly connected to what Hugo Wagner is doing, it's going to get pretty dangerous for anyone getting in their way."

"If the Hidden Empire actually exists, it adds a whole new dimension to the situation," Ben said. "Let's hope we can get a lot of things figured out real soon and then take the necessary actions."

****

At eight o'clock local time the next morning in his new hi-tech fortress in a mountainous region in southern Germany, Hugo Wagner sat in one of the four chairs in the center portion of the control room.

Oleg and Wan sat in two of the other chairs.

Hugo placed the red dot from his laser pointer on the image showing the new office building to support their global financial operations in the Jacksonville area. The office was built to facilitate closer coordination of all the international monetary institutions.

"With our superior spying technology, we know our new office is going to get a visit from a group containing Baker and Gibson in the next few days." Hugo glanced at Oleg and Wan. "We need to decide what we want to do."

"I don't think we should overreact," Oleg said. "We can wait a bit and see what happens. Our satellites are in place all over the world, and our other spying equipment is fully functional. We'll know instantly if we need to be in a big rush to eliminate an immediate threat."

Wan nodded. "Since we have over ten thousand programs running at the same time on the quantum computer, and each one searches for specific things we want to know, we get notified instantly."

Hugo laughed. "With our intelligence and hi-tech capability, we're definitely going to know everything and we're going to be impossible to stop."

"And speaking of being impossible to stop, are there any things we still need to do to insure the money keeps coming in?" Oleg asked.

Hugo glanced at Wan. "You're our financial expert. Do you recommend anything more than what we've already done?"

"Nothing more right now," Wan said. "We've already set up the mechanism to insure we'll continue to receive our share of the money from the activity by the Mexican Drug Cartels, and we can hack into any bank in the world anytime we want to."

Hugo nodded. "Since Carmen and Hector are still in jail, it's good we made preparations to continue to receive our money. We had good foresight."

"Think we should get them out of jail?" Oleg asked. "We can do that pretty easily."

"Yeah, but we really don't need them anymore," Hugo said. "The payoff system we set up to run on automatic is functioning very well. The cartels are still sending money to the designated accounts like they were while Carmen and Hector were running things."

Leaning forward, Wan looked at both Hugo and Oleg. "What if the cartel leaders all find out both Carmen and Hector are in jail and are no longer running the drug trafficking operation?"

"Yeah," Oleg said, looking at Hugo. "They're paying for Carmen and Hector to be active in protecting them from the Mexican Government. They expect all the right people to be paid off when necessary and that situation changes over time. It needs to be actively managed." He shrugged. "Besides, the money we'll spend to pay all the right people to get them released is no issue for us."

Hugo rubbed his chin.

There was a brief silence.

Oleg stared at Hugo. "Well?"

"You have a good point and they could also be useful in eliminating Baker and Gibson," Hugo said. "We'll get them out of jail and put them back to work."

Chapter 5

Later that afternoon, Ben called a group together for more discussion.

Matt, Ralph, Justin, Vince, Judy, Todd, and Steve sat with Ben at the large table in the main conference room at the Jacksonville FBI Headquarters.

"Well, NSA has intercepted some more calls and NRO has sent more images," Ben said. "We have even more information to discuss, and I thought we should do it quickly." He scanned the faces around the table. "Russia developed a huge underwater missile carrying a nuclear warhead. They named the missile 'Poseidon.' It is sixty-five feet long and six point five feet wide. The warhead is a large thermonuclear bomb capable of creating a radioactive tsunami to swamp any targeted coastal city in the United States."

"How big is the warhead?" Matt asked.

"The original one was two megatons, but that has changed since China is now involved," Ben said. "With China's boost to their technology, the Russians now have one that's five megatons and they're working on making it one hundred megatons."

Matt narrowed his eyes. "That's pretty powerful considering the first atomic bomb the United States dropped on Hiroshima in Japan during World War II was only one point five megatons. And the second one they dropped on Nagasaki was only two megatons."

Todd leaned forward. "And they were two different bombs. The first one was a uranium bomb they labeled 'Little Boy' to give it a name. The second one, called 'Fat Man,' was a plutonium bomb."

Matt was accustomed to Todd always giving additional facts about things they were discussing. Sometimes the facts were useful, sometimes not. But they were usually interesting.

"Chinese experts have been working with Russian experts to develop an even bigger bomb with a better navigation system," Ben said. "The new Poseidon missile they've developed is eighty feet long and eight feet wide. It's designed to carry a warhead of up to one hundred megatons of explosive power and it has a nuclear navigation system to improve its capability to maneuver better in many ways."

"Can you give us some more details on that?" Ralph asked.

"FBI experts tell me the newest version can travel underwater at a speed of eighty miles an hour," Ben said. "That's faster than America's nuclear-powered attack-submarines and also their anti-ship missiles." He narrowed his eyes. "The new version of the Poseidon missiles can also travel at a depth of three thousand two hundred eighty feet. That's lower than any of our American submarines can go. China and Russia jointly call it their Tsunami Apocalypse Torpedo. Since it's powered by a miniature nuclear reactor, it effectively has unlimited range."

Ralph shook his head slowly. "That's scary."

"And there's more," Ben said. "Their engineers have added ramjet engines and have been able to create a bubble of gas for the missile to travel in. This reduces friction with the water and they've been able to improve the speed to more than two hundred miles per hour."

"Do you think this is something we need to be concerned with right now?" Matt asked.

"Yeah, according to some recent conversations NSA intercepted, Hugo Wagner has purchased some of them for his inventory." Ben exhaled slowly. "China is now supplying all the technology for these underwater missiles. Their team, who developed the Sunway Taihulight supercomputer, also developed a miniature version of a quantum computer to serve as the navigational system for them. We might have some big things to worry about. Our experts are working to get us some more information."

"Do you have a new point to make?" Ralph asked.

"Just that Hugo now can launch a missile toward any site he chooses to destroy," Ben said. "Our CIA and the Germans need to redouble their efforts to work closely together to shut him down as soon as possible."

Todd nodded. "Hugo is probably using a quantum computer to analyze mountains of data as he evaluates all of his options and develops the next steps in his conquest strategy."

"Yeah, and we need to eliminate the threats from Hugo and his group for a lot of reasons," Ben said. "They can use the quantum computer to hack into many of our information systems. With all that speed, a quantum computer can bypass the safeguards in most of those systems."

"Do we know if they've hacked into any of our banking systems and stolen any of our money yet?" Judy asked.

"We know they've tried to hack into some of our Federal Reserve banks," Ben said, "but we have quantum computers too. We've been using them for defense and so far we've been able to prevent any successful attacks. There are a lot of people working on defending all of our financial systems from future hacking attempts. All the other intelligence agencies are working with us on that."

Ben narrowed his eyes as he looked around the table.

"Thanks to Todd and Steve, we already have an excellent security system at Tuxtun," Ralph said. "Also Matt and I both have upgraded our home systems along with the rest of our employees. I don't think we can improve our security anymore at present."

Vince nodded and motioned toward Justin. "That's the same with us."

Matt looked at Ben. "Do you have any specific recommendations for us right now?"

"We all need to stay on high alert. Looks like we're going to have a lot more challenges to deal with very soon." Ben tightened his jaw and gave a slight shrug. "We'll see how things develop as we go forward."

****

The next morning in his headquarters in southern Germany, Hugo Wagner, Oleg Titov, and Wan Lu sat at the doughnut-shaped round table in the middle of their hi-tech control room.

"Are you ready to move forward with our next step?" Hugo asked, looking at his cohorts.

Wan narrowed his eyes. "I assume that's eliminating Baker and Gibson."

"You're correct in your assumption." Hugo flashed

a big smile. "I've decided the sooner we get them out of our way, the better. They've been a huge nuisance, and I find that unsettling. I don't want that hanging over me."

"What's your initial strategy going to be?" Oleg asked.

"I think we should immediately get some more good assassins on our payroll and continue evaluating the situation at Tuxtun," Hugo said. "After we hire them, we should give the assassins a few days to get prepared. It would be foolish to rush and make a big mistake." He looked at Oleg. "Have you made sure you're set up to pay your Russian assassins without the funds being traceable?"

"Yes," Oleg replied instantly. "We have a lot of accounts established just for that. We put in some extra twists to keep them well-disguised. All the money is routed through shell companies who use multiple layers of transactions embedded in different facets of the World Bank."

"Good," Hugo said. "And we have a lot of options other than assassins we can use." He made a circular gesture covering the room. "With all the capability we have here, we can choose between a huge assortment of methods."

Wan and Oleg both nodded.

Hugo leaned toward Oleg. "Have you heard from the Kremlin recently?"

"I was getting ready to tell you," Oleg said. "They'll ship us two Poseidon missiles as soon as you give them all the delivery instructions. Our location is much better protected than any others they ship to."

Hugo nodded slowly. "And what's the status of the

assassins you requested yesterday?"

"My contacts in the Kremlin are in the process of selecting two more of their best ones to send us," Oleg said.

Hugo narrowed his eyes. "Tell them they need to speed it up."

Oleg gave a thumbs-up. "They already have one, Ludvig Kats. He's among their best and he's already in the United States. They told me they would get back to me sometime today to coordinate the details."

"What's his current location?" Hugo asked.

"He's in Miami," Oleg said. "He can be in Jacksonville tomorrow."

Hugo rubbed his chin. "Since he's one of Russia's best, we'll plan to use him quickly."

"Exactly what do you have in mind?" Oleg asked.

"I'll get to that in a few moments," Hugo said. "Due to our previous encounters with Baker and Gibson, we have a pretty good profile on each of them. Baker is a slightly better warrior."

"Are you going after him first?" Wan asked.

Hugo shrugged. "They're usually together. We'll see how things work out. We have detailed information about their schedules and office hours."

"Did we get the information from our moles in Washington?" Oleg asked.

Hugo grinned. "Our quantum computer gathered all of it." He stared at Oleg for a moment. "Do you think Ludvig can eliminate Baker in a one-on-one confrontation?"

"Remember, Ludvig's one of our best," Oleg said.

"You didn't answer my question."

With a sweeping gesture, Oleg lifted both hands in

the air as he thrust his chin out. "Of course he can handle Baker."

"Baker has never lost an encounter with any of your previous assassins and you told us they were the best you had," Wan said. He turned slightly and stared at Oleg.

Oleg tilted his head and stared back at Wan. "Remember, Baker always had some help around." He hesitated a moment and then leaned toward Wan. "I'm confident Ludvig can get the job done."

"Gibson is almost always with Baker and he's good too," Wan said. "Baker will still have some help around."

Oleg nodded. "We'll consider that and we'll have a plan that will work this time. We will definitely eliminate Baker and probably Gibson too."

Wan's eyes narrowed. "Maybe using a sniper to shoot both of them as they're leaving the Tuxtun offices would be our smartest move."

"Remember, we got the information a while back from our quantum computer that using a sniper at Tuxtun won't work," Oleg said. "Tuxtun has technology that will sound an alarm if a rifle is within four hundred yards of the property."

"Are you sure that's still the case?" Hugo asked.

"I'll check on that again later," Oleg said. "Right now I'll check with Ludvig and plan for him to confront Baker as soon as we work out the best timing, if that's okay with you."

Hugo nodded slowly as he scanned the multiple displays covering the circular wall. "The programming for the quantum computer seems to be working to perfection. We have a ton of information about a lot of things that concern us." He focused the red dot from his pointer on some data. "Note the security Tuxtun has installed for detecting snipers is still in place."

Oleg and Wan both nodded.

Hugo now focused the red dot on some information displayed on one of the screens. "There's the schedule information for both Baker and Gibson for the next week. We should be able to determine the best timing very quickly. We don't really need the moles, but it's still good to keep them available. Sometimes they might know something we haven't yet found with the AI."

"We shouldn't discard the idea of having a sniper pick both of them off at some location," Wan said. "If Gibson stays alive, he can still become a big problem. Getting rid of both of them at the same time will be a great thing for us."

Hugo pursed his lips and nodded slowly. "We'll have some expert snipers available real soon. Two German assassins I plan to add to our team have superior skills in that regard." He looked at Wan. "If we don't eliminate Baker and Gibson in the next day or so, that might prove to be the best strategy. We'll keep that in mind and ambush them when they're away from their offices. Right now, let's try to agree on what our next global action should be for moving us forward in our quest to conquer the world."

Each man raised his right fist high in the air.

****

In an elaborate castle in Switzerland, three elderly men were sitting in a plush lounge area.

None of them owned the castle, their organization did. It was where they met when they needed to discuss some important things. They were members of the Illuminati, a secret society that controlled a lot of world events.

The castle was located about twenty miles east of Zurich.

None of them knew the real names of the others. Each addressed his cohorts with an assigned codename adapted from the names of the mythical Greek, Roman, and Norse Gods.

The names Zeus, Jupiter, and Odin were reserved for the three most powerful global leaders. The Illuminati demonstrated remarkable efficiency in its operations, with a division into three significant global segments. Each of the global leaders supervised one of the segments.

The oldest man at the meeting, who had the code name of Vulcan, filled his pipe with his favorite almond-blend tobacco. Smoking helped him relax. After lighting his pipe and taking a puff, he looked at the other two men.

Vulcan noted the man who had the code name of Neptune was still in the process of filling his pipe with what Vulcan knew was cherry-blend tobacco. They were both heavy smokers, and they each had their favorite tobacco.

Neptune flicked his lighter and positioned the flame. While taking a few puffs to get his pipe going, he glanced toward his team leader, Vulcan.

The third man, code name Apollo, didn't smoke, but he was in the process of adjusting the cushion in the chair he was sitting in.

Vulcan contemplated the situation they were going to discuss as he waited for his cohorts to get settled.

Their multiple international businesses were all booming, and the money was pouring in.

However, it looked like Hugo Wagner was going to interfere with the money flow in several ways. He might need to be eliminated and his entire operation destroyed. They would discuss that.

The three men were of different nationalities but they all were united by a strong passion to support the Illuminati.

When his two partners seemed to get comfortable, Vulcan asked, "Since this is our first meeting in a month, does anyone have an urgent topic to discuss?" He leaned forward.

Neptune immediately shook his head as he slowly took a large puff from his pipe. He fixed his gaze on Vulcan. "I'm sure you have one. Go ahead and get us started."

Turning slightly, Vulcan looked at the nonsmoker and asked, "How about you, Apollo? Do you have any subject you think we need to discuss?"

Apollo looked directly at Vulcan. "What are you worried about?"

"Why do you think I'm worried?"

"Neptune and I both know you worry a lot. I figure something must be on your mind for you to suddenly call this meeting. You usually give us more time to plan our trip over here."

"There are several things I want to mention. We can decide if any of them need discussion," Vulcan said. "First of all, the Russian KGB now has a fully operational spy base set up in Nicaragua."

"When did you find out?" Apollo asked.

"Thor contacted me early this morning," Vulcan

said. "He utilized the normal method for sending me the message. No way could it be intercepted."

"The Russians still have spy bases in Venezuela, Argentina, and several other places on that side of the globe, don't they?" Neptune asked.

Vulcan nodded. "This new one in Nicaragua is more advanced and it's another step to increase Russian capability in the western hemisphere as they move toward their goal of world domination, which we don't oppose since the KGB is the action arm of the Illuminati."

"Did Thor have any other news?" Apollo asked.

"The Kremlin is getting more concerned that Hugo Wagner is going to use a nuclear weapon to wipe out part of the United States and completely disable their economy," Vulcan said.

Apollo narrowed his eyes. "That will certainly disrupt the global money flow we depend on to accomplish our goals. We can't allow that."

Neptune gave a quick nod.

"That's a big reason we're having this meeting," Vulcan said. "Also, Hugo seems to be continuing his plan to capture all the gold supply in the United States even after he was warned last year specifically about that."

"Do we need to do something soon about any of these things?" Apollo asked.

"We don't yet have any new mission ourselves but Thor told me our bosses are discussing the best action to take," Vulcan said. "He mentioned they'll probably try to communicate with Hugo again and ask him to change his plans before they take any drastic action against him."

"What type of drastic action?" Neptune asked.

"Thor told me they might decide to eliminate him and his entire operation," Vulcan said. "We have that capability when we need to use it."

"And Thor's boss is the one who gave him all the information regarding the concern about Hugo Wagner and the possible action we might take?" Neptune asked.

"Of course, that's the way things work with us." Vulcan took a long slow puff on his pipe. "We always use the chain of command to maintain the utmost secrecy."

Neptune gave a slight shrug. "I know that. I just wanted to be absolutely sure in this case. It looks like we're getting into some very dangerous waters here and we have to make sure we don't assume anything and miss some important details."

Vulcan nodded. "I don't blame you for wanting to clarify. We can't afford any mistakes. We need to get some big things done and we want to remain invisible to the public while we do them." He narrowed his eyes. "Having the world constantly disrupted helps us to maintain our secrecy and Hugo has been useful in contributing to that, but we can't allow him to go too far and interfere with any of our necessary processes." He fixed his gaze on both Neptune and Apollo. "I'll keep you informed. We'll probably have another meeting soon."

Chapter 6

In the main conference room at Tuxtun, Matt and Ralph sat at the large conference table with Judy, Todd, and Steve.

"Looks like we're going to have some big problems to resolve real soon," Ralph said. "We need to stay closely coordinated. So I thought we should have this meeting to compare notes and make sure we're all as up-to-date as possible on events that could affect us." He scanned the faces around the table.

Everyone nodded.

Ralph gestured to Judy. "I think you have some new information."

"The International Acceptance Bank of New York had a huge number of transactions last week," Judy said. "I keep up with those types of things and I think that's significant."

"Why do you think that?" Matt asked.

Judy leaned forward and kept her gaze locked on Matt. "I'm a big proponent of following the money. Using an acceptance bank to deliver money to the right people creates another layer of secrecy. My guess is that a lot of money has just been delivered and the people who are sending it want the transactions to be as inconspicuous as possible."

"Can you explain acceptance banking for us?" Matt asked, returning Judy's stare.

Judy gave a slight shrug. "The way it works in certain cases is complicated and difficult to explain simply, but I'll give it a try." She pressed her lips together for a moment. "Acceptance banking is basically a process of guaranteeing repayments of loans. In the broader sense of things, I've concluded it's another way of delivering money to people who you want to remain in the background as much as possible."

"That's not very clear," Ralph said.

Judy grunted. "I mentioned it could be a complicated process." She hesitated for a few seconds. "Maybe a little background will help"

There was a brief silence.

"Our Federal Reserve System was created in 1913," Judy said. After a few years of creating money out of nothing, the founders of the Federal Reserve System decided they needed this bank. One of the founders took the initiative and created the International Acceptance Bank of New York in 1921."

"I've never heard of it," Matt said. "But I'm familiar with a lot of other entities in the global monetary flow."

Judy nodded. "As more time passed, the powers behind all the global money flow found out they needed the World Bank, the IMF, and the WTO too. These institutions were added to the global monetary system much later on." She shrugged. "But let's not get off the main subject. Let's get back to thinking about why the International Acceptance Bank of New York just had a huge increase in transactions."

"I still don't understand the connection between the increase in transactions and what we're concerned about regarding Hugo Wagner," Steve said, "and maybe regarding the Hidden Empire too."

"Let's just say this additional process in the global money flow further legitimizes things and helps move large amounts of money to the intended destinations, to both organizations and people." Judy gestured toward Todd. "He and I both think a lot of people in the shadows have just been paid off and many of those people could be assassins."

Todd nodded. "Obviously, the people making the payments don't want the money trail to be discovered, but Judy and I keep a sharp lookout for any big changes in any element of the global money flow."

Ralph scanned the faces around the table. "There's a good chance we'll benefit from this knowledge in the future as we move forward with all of our global business issues. I think it will be good to go a little deeper on this general subject before we stop. I'm curious as to how the Hidden Empire is funded." He gestured toward Judy and Todd.

"The additional details I can make you aware of will make things even more complicated," Judy said.

Ralph shrugged. "Go ahead. We can all handle it."

"There are many reasons why so many worldwide payments remain hidden," Judy said. "The more Todd and I dug into this, the more entangled everything got."

Todd nodded. "We got some good training by trying to trace the money Hugo Wagner was paying various organizations and people to help further his objectives, but it was nothing like what we've run into by trying to gain some insight into how the Hidden Empire's money flow works."

"Just summarize it for us," Ralph said. "We don't need all the details."

"We now know the Hidden Empire exists and we know they have a system of paying organizations and people just like Hugo Wagner does," Judy said, "except the Hidden Empire doesn't need to set up shell companies to make their system work. They already have powerful people in the right positions in all the global monetary institutions to make everything work the way they need it to."

Todd nodded. "And we know they'll eliminate anyone who interferes with it." He clenched his jaw. "The team of financial experts we're working with can't untangle the mass of information we've collected fast enough to make any quick progress. We estimate it will take over a hundred years just to untangle what we have now. It's no wonder the Hidden Empire can remain invisible."

Ralph gave a short laugh. "Well, I don't think you and Judy will need to spend much more of your time on that, anyway. After this discussion, you can go back to spending most of your time on our own finances."

"We will," Judy said. "But Todd and I each have a strong personal desire to unravel the global money flow of the Hidden Empire and understand it." She shrugged. "That's not likely to happen but we would like to spend a little more time developing a better understanding of the big picture."

"And those of us who're curious about it will enjoy hearing yours and Todd's summary." Matt smiled and looked at Ralph.

Ralph gestured to Judy. "All right, go ahead."

"Well let's continue with a few more basic facts to give this some perspective. Some of this will be a brief review of things Todd and I have mentioned before and some of it will be new," Judy said. "The International Acceptance Bank of New York was established in 1921 to provide some necessary adjustments to the system the Hidden Empire was setting up. That worked well enough for a while because the system didn't need to be too sophisticated back in those days."

Todd nodded. "In 1930, the powerful people who were making a lot of money from this system decided they needed another enhancement so they created the Bank for International Settlements (BIS) in Basel, Switzerland. This new bank provided a multitude of new services and promoted cooperation among central banks."

"Next, the Federal Reserve created the Federal Open Market Committee (FOMC) in 1933," Judy said. "The first branch of the World Bank, the International Bank for Reconstruction and Development (IBRD) was created in 1944 along with the International Monetary Fund (IMF). Both were for the purpose of rebuilding after World War II. The headquarters for both occupies a square block along Pennsylvania Avenue two blocks west of the White House."

Todd leaned forward. "The other four branches of the World Bank were added later. The International Finance Corporation (IFC) was added in 1956 and the International Development Association (IDA) was added in 1960. The IFC is the private-sector arm of the World Bank and gives it a lot more freedom for money distribution among private entities."

"The Institute of International Finance (IIF), which is a separate entity from the World Bank, was created in 1983," Judy said. "The fifth branch of the World Bank was added in 1988. That was the Multilateral

Investment Guarantee Agency (MIGA)."

"And finally, the World Trade Organization (WTO) was created in Geneva, Switzerland in 1995," Todd added. "And that's the overall structure we're looking at. The billions of transactions daily among the various entities are intertwined in a complex manner."

Ralph laughed. "That's a lot more to think about. You're right about it being even more complicated." His gaze took in both Judy and Todd. "Do you have much more to tell us?"

"Just a little bit more and then we'll wrap it up," Judy said. "Most of the additions to the global monetary system over the years had a lot to do with investments and credit. A lot of money could be made by the owners of various aspects of the global monetary system by charging fees to guarantee loans."

Matt gave a short laugh. "Yeah, like you mentioned earlier, charging fees to guarantee loans was recognized by the creators of the Federal Reserve as a great way to make more money. When they created the International Acceptance Bank of New York they started taking advantage of that."

"When the crew on Jekyll Island envisioned setting up the Federal Reserve they somehow overlooked that way to make money or they couldn't easily incorporate it into what they set up in 1913." Judy shrugged. "Anyway, they made the adjustment."

"And from what you and Todd outlined just now, the powers in the global monetary system have continued to make similar adjustments over the years," Matt said.

Judy and Todd nodded.

Ralph leaned toward them. "Thanks for your

research. I think we can be certain the Hidden Empire exists and will take action when anyone threatens their operation."

"It's good to keep a general knowledge of what Judy and Todd just explained in mind," Matt said. "If we continue to grow crops in Mexico we're almost certain to have problems with cartels that use parts of the same system. We'll continue to have problems with Hugo too but I think we're well prepared for both of those. What we don't want is to have problems with the Hidden Empire so we don't want to do something to hamper their operations."

Ralph leaned forward. "Yep, we need to keep a basic understanding of the full financial environment we're maneuvering around in. If we're careful, we shouldn't become a problem for them. We don't plan to work toward changing anything in the global monetary system. That will be someone else's job."

Everyone gave a thumbs-up.

After a brief hesitation, Ralph said, "We have a complex tangle of items and it's a good idea to thoroughly understand everything before we make any moves." He gestured toward Judy and Todd. "You've briefed me a few times on some other related items Go ahead and give us a few more details on the depth of this thing."

"Are any of you familiar with the Bilderberg Group?" Todd asked.

Matt didn't comment. He had heard the name, but he knew nothing about them.

Ralph and Steve also remained silent.

"They have meetings around the world," Todd said. "And the meetings are closed to the public. They have an annual, unofficial, invitation-only conference of around hundred fifty people from North America and Western Europe. About a third of them are from government and the rest are from finance, industry, and education. All, of course, are people of influence."

"What do they do at the conference?" Matt asked.

"In broad terms, they discuss major problems facing the United States and Western Europe," Todd said, "and then come up with action plans." He gave a small grin. "Or, at least, that's what they advertise."

"Do you have any specifics on the action plans?" Ralph asked.

"I've never been able to get any details," Todd said. "They keep everything very secretive and they seem to have powerful resources at their disposal to be able to do that."

"Do you have any details on the nature of these resources?" Ralph asked.

"Judy and I have worked on that, but, so far, we just have odds and ends," Todd said. "Much is speculation based on a few facts. There are thousands of pieces to the puzzle."

Ralph's gaze took in both Todd and Judy. "Tell us what you know."

"Academia seems to be a big player," Judy said. "Georgetown's Institute for the Study of Diplomacy is part of that picture. Princeton, Yale, and Harvard are also involved." She then leaned forward and gave a detailed explanation. When she finished, there were several minutes of silence.

"When the Pope abolished the Knights Templar, they joined the Free Masons, right?" Matt asked.

"No one is sure about the origin of the Free

Masons, but there's a lot of evidence their inner circle formed the group known as the Illuminati," Todd said. "Another name for the Illuminati is The Enlightened Ones."

"You mentioned they want a one-world government and a religion that controls the population?" Ralph asked.

"That's correct," Todd said. "They want to abolish private property."

There was another period of silence.

"I find it disturbing the Order of Skull & Bones at Yale is believed to have some connection to the Illuminati," Ralph said. "We've had at least two presidents who were members."

Todd rubbed his chin. "I don't know much about them right now, but I know the Bilderberg Group and the owners of the Federal Reserve are believed to be active in the overall power structure of the Illuminati."

"Especially the owners of the Federal Reserve," Judy said. "I've found some additional financial information I need to research. I'll have more to say about that later."

"Do you think the Russian government is involved in this?" Matt asked.

"That's for sure," Todd said. "There's a lot of evidence that heads of the Illuminati control the Russian KGB. It's likely the leaders of the KGB compose part of the Hidden Empire. They probably provide a hit squad when one is needed."

Matt scanned the faces around the table. "So what do we do next?"

"There's another item I haven't mentioned that might influence what decision we make," Todd said.

"During our latest research, we discovered a couple of new Hispanic assassins who work for Carmen Vargas and Hector Medina."

"Aren't Vargas and Medina still in jail?" Ralph asked.

Todd pursed his lips and shook his head slowly. "They're free now. Someone put up ten million dollars to get them out. The source of that money is well hidden. Judy and I are still working on it. The two assassins are Ricardo Sanchez and Carlos Torres."

Matt looked at Todd and Judy. "Should we expect some kind of attack in the next few days?"

"That's certainly a possibility," Todd said. "Judy and I will catalog our findings in the threat matrix we're putting together."

Judy nodded. "We have a huge maze of items that might need to be added to our threat matrix. We need to organize it well for it to be useful."

"We certainly need to stay on top of what's going on," Ralph said. "I'm glad Matt and I got the extra weapons training recently." He narrowed his eyes as his gaze focused on Todd and Judy. "Do you think the Federal Reserve is part of the Illuminati?"

Todd and Judy both gave him a questioning look.

"I'm wondering about the international powers in the ownership behind the Federal Reserve," Ralph said. "I've heard they've knocked off a couple of Presidents and tried to knock off a few more. If they get irritated about your investigations they might decide to retaliate."

Todd gave a slow nod. "You have a point. Most owners of the Federal Reserve can be classified as international powers."

"So you think they might be part of the Illuminati?" Ralph asked.

"That would be a logical deduction." Todd's gaze took in both Ralph and Matt. "It looks like we've again become immersed in a very complex situation."

"We survived everything before," Matt said. "We can do it again."

"That's true but we're still dealing with some extremely dangerous people." Steve focused his gaze directly on Matt and Ralph. "We all need to take every precaution we can but I think you two will be the main targets of any assassins who show up."

"Ben has already scheduled some more weapons training for Ralph and me at the new FBI facility here in Jacksonville," Matt said. "We're going tomorrow morning. Apparently, he agrees with what you just alluded to."

Chapter 7

The next morning Ralph and Matt each wore a sports coat with casual clothes and carried a Glock 19 in a holster attached to the belt toward the back of the right hip.

Standing inside the large dome, which housed the new FBI weapons training center in the Jacksonville area, they looked at a replica of a city street that stretched before them.

Everything was dark except for a few streetlights, a good simulation of night conditions.

From their previous training sessions, Matt and Ralph already knew this facility simulated all day and night conditions, including wind and rain.

Due to the threats they were facing, Matt figured Ben had requested an extra tough routine for them to complete today.

Matt watched a man, who looked like a seasoned military veteran, walk toward them. He was obviously the instructor.

Probably Special Forces, Matt thought.

"In this session, we'll get some city-street action for both day and night conditions." The instructor studied Matt and Ralph for a moment. "Ben asked me to upgrade your training to our top level. It's going to be challenging. You ready to tackle this?"

"I think we're both as ready as we'll ever be," Matt

said.

The instructor looked at Ralph.

Ralph nodded. "I'm okay with it."

The instructor narrowed his eyes. "You'll do the pistol training first and I hope you do better than the other participants who've gone through this particular segment. You'll need to make good judgments and you'll need to draw fast. The targets will only be exposed for one second."

Matt and Ralph both nodded.

"Do you have any questions?" the instructor asked.

Matt and Ralph remained silent.

"Let's see how well you can handle this first exercise. One of you should move to the left side of the street, the other to the right."

When Matt and Ralph started walking, the instructor turned and climbed the steps to a platform 30 feet high.

Matt stood on the right side of the street, Ralph on the left side.

The high-intensity streetlights dimmed. Faint silhouettes of buildings loomed around them. A fine mist fell from the simulated night sky.

Matt and Ralph moved forward along the dimly lit street. Matt scanned the training area, the size of a city block. A target popped up to his right. He drew fast and fired. The target went down. For several minutes, he and Ralph picked off targets while they both moved down the street.

Staying alert, Matt saw targets on both sides of the street. He shot all of them. He noted Ralph was doing a lot of firing too.

"Hold it," a voice from the darkness shouted.

As bright light flooded the area, the instructor hurried down from the platform and over to where Matt stood.

The instructor gestured for Ralph to join them.

"We're not in the deep woods." The instructor glared at both of his students. "City streets are different. You're making too many mistakes. You need to do better or you're going to die."

Both Matt and Ralph stared at the instructor and remained silent.

The instructor shook his head slowly and pursed his lips. "You've both been through this before. For experienced warriors, this was a piss-poor effort if I ever saw one."

"What are you talking about? Ralph asked. "We got all of the targets."

Matt nodded. "And we got them fast too."

"Neither of you saw that last target." Disgust covered the instructor's face. "In real life, you'd be dead."

Matt was suspicious the instructor was just taunting them. He glanced at Ralph who also looked skeptical.

"When you start again, move your head from side to side," the instructor said. "You can best detect movement out of the corners of your eyes."

Ralph glanced at the instructor and said, "That last target must have been well hidden."

"A little more than usual but no more than an expert assassin you would encounter in a downtown setting." The instructor spat out the words as he glared at them.

Matt and Ralph didn't comment.

"Start scanning properly if you want to stay alive."

The instructor scolded. "In this type of situation, keep rotating your head. That might save your life, unless you screw something else up."

Matt nodded. So did Ralph.

"Ben told me you're both among the best gunmen who've ever worked with him," the instructor said. "But you both would have died if you had been in a real situation like this against expert assassins." The instructor turned and stomped off, glaring back over his shoulder. "None of us in law enforcement want you to die so let's see some improvement."

After climbing to the platform, the instructor shouted, "This has been a damned dismal performance up to this point for supposed experts."

The instructor was right about one thing for sure, Matt thought. They needed to improve their skill in this particular scenario.

"The ability to execute a fast draw from a hidden holster will come in handy in many real-life situations," the instructor said. "You need to be able to execute the whole exercise skillfully."

Matt and Ralph didn't comment

The lights dimmed.

While turning his head from side to side, Matt moved forward through the fine mist. Determined to improve, he scanned the area. There, to his right, on the rooftop. He drew and fired. The target went down.

He continued for several minutes, eliminating target after target.

Reloading quickly was part of the exercise. Matt carried four extra full magazines. He knew after he and Ralph each fired seventy-five shots, there would be a break in the action and they would each receive five new magazines.

After one of the breaks, the simulation shifted to daytime conditions.

The additional practice lasted two more hours before the instructor called a halt and descended from the platform.

Matt and Ralph moved to the middle of the street and watched the instructor approach.

"If you can maintain the skill level you've reached, both of you have a reasonable chance to stay alive," the instructor said. He gave a slight shrug. "Of course your staying alive will also depend on the skill level of your opponents."

"How do we compare to your other students who've completed this course?" Ralph asked.

"You're the best, but that doesn't mean you'll stay alive against highly talented opponents," the instructor said. "You have to always think there are guys you'll run into who're better than you are. That's a primary reason you have to always put all of your effort into getting better every time you get some more training."

Matt shared the instructor's opinion about them being the best and he was always going to put out his best effort to improve. He knew Ralph had the same thinking. They had been through a lot of tough situations together and, at least so far, they had survived.

The instructor studied them for a moment. "It's good you improved and did okay on this part. I'm told you'll need to keep applying these skills as you go forward in your work." He stared at them for a moment more. "Now go change clothes for the next part."

A few minutes later, Matt and Ralph, each wearing

SWAT team gear, stood ready to continue the training.

"This next segment has been redone to be a lot more difficult. You ready?" the instructor asked.

"Of course we're ready," Matt said matter-of-factly, trying not to sound smarty.

Ralph nodded.

The instructor thrust out his chin. "I just hope you can do better than the other participants. They thought they were ready too. This next one is much tougher than anyone expects." He handed both of them a rifle with a short stock and two pistol grips. "This is a SIG 556. It uses NATO 5.56mm rounds and can fire 900 rounds per minute. It has a thirty-round magazine."

Even though he had used it before, Matt held the compact rifle level and juggled it. Ralph did the same.

"It weighs seven point eight pounds." The instructor pursed his lips. "It's exactly thirty-seven inches long. Good weapon to use at night. Flash suppressors disperse the gas venting from the barrel, diffusing its brightness. Helps conceal your position. A good marksman can hit a four-inch square target at four hundred yards with it."

Matt made no comment. He had heard this before. He figured the instructor had a set speech he used every time.

Ralph also did not comment as he nodded at the instructor.

"We're now using this weapon in many intelligence and law-enforcement agencies," The instructor said. "You'll get some more city street action in nighttime conditions and then you'll go to the outdoor scenarios, any questions?"

Matt and Ralph remained silent.

The instructor checked his watch. "Okay, let's see how well you can use it. Set it for semi-automatic fire." After waving them to their starting positions, he turned and climbed to the high platform.

This time Ralph stood on the right side of the street.

Matt stood on the left side.

The high-intensity streetlights dimmed.

Faint silhouettes of buildings loomed around them.

A fine mist fell from the simulated night sky as Matt and Ralph moved forward along the dark street.

Matt held his silenced SIG 556 rifle in a ready position and scanned the training area. A target popped up to his left. He fired and hit it.

For several minutes, he and Ralph picked off targets while they both moved down the street.

Staying alert, Matt saw a lot of targets pop up. He shot at all of them but he wasn't sure whether he hit them or not. They might have gone down automatically.

"Hold it," a voice from the darkness shouted. As bright light flooded the area, the instructor hurried down from the platform and over to where Matt was standing.

The instructor gestured to Ralph to join them.

"What's wrong?" Matt asked.

"A lot of things," the instructor said. "Keep performing like this and you'll get your ass shot off for sure by assassins who're highly skilled with automatic rifles." He scowled. "You have a good weapon, use it. That applies to both of you." He turned and stomped off, glaring back over his shoulder. "Now let's see some real improvement."

"Can you name something specific we're doing

wrong?" Ralph asked.

"For one thing, you need to improve your response time for identifying the target." The instructor turned and walked back toward the platform. "This has been a dismal performance so far."

Matt figured the instructor was just following a script to keep them motivated to perform as well as they could. That was okay with him. He figured it was okay with Ralph too. They needed to be as sharp as possible anytime they encountered professional assassins.

The lights dimmed and the simulated weather got worse.

While turning his head from side to side, Matt moved forward through heavy rain.

Determined to improve, Matt kept his SIG 556 ready.

To his left, on the rooftop, another target, Matt fired, got it. Moving forward, he hit target after target. He knew he had hit them because they had all gone down instantly.

Matt felt he had made some improvement.

After nailing twenty more targets in a variety of locations—rooftops, alleys, second-story windows, doorways—Matt felt he had mastered this exercise. Every target had gone down fast.

"Halt," a familiar voice shouted.

Lights came on. The instructor strolled toward them. "Better." He gave a half smile. "Both of you did okay for this part." He studied them for a moment. "We'll move to the deep-woods section."

After they moved to the deep-woods section of the massive training facility, they completed two grueling hours of additional practice.

During the wrap-up, the instructor told them they were the best of everyone who had gone through this set of exercises so far and, if they maintained their sharpness, they should be good enough to handle their assignments.

Matt shared the instructor's opinion. He noted Ralph also appeared confident.

The instructor studied them for a moment. "It's good you did okay. I'm told you'll probably need to apply these skills soon. Good luck."

Ralph and Matt both nodded.

Before he turned away, the instructor said, "Steve, Ben, Justin, and Vince are all scheduled to go through the same training you just completed. Looks like someone expects things to be heating up real soon."

Chapter 8

In southern Germany, Hugo Wagner, Oleg Titov, and Wan Lu sat in their hi-tech control room at their fortress.

Hugo scanned the multiple displays on the circular wall and focused his laser pointer on an area in Jacksonville.

Both Oleg and Wan studied the information around the area of the red dot and waited for Hugo to comment.

"The sooner we get Baker and Gibson out of our way the better," Hugo said. "We're ready to move and we now have more backup." He looked at Oleg. "I think we should use Ricardo Sanchez and Carlos Torres to back up Ludvig. They're in the area."

"Why do you still insist he has backup?" Oleg asked.

"I want to be sure we get the job done as soon as possible."

Oleg leaned forward. "I told you Ludvig was our best."

"It never hurts to have overwhelming odds."

Oleg narrowed his eyes. "Let's give Ludvig his chance. I'm sure he can handle it."

Hugo hesitated a moment and gave a slow nod. He glanced at Wan. "You're our financial expert. Have you checked everything thoroughly to make sure we can pay all of our assassins without the funds being traceable?"

"Yes," Wan said. "Oleg was correct when he told us additional accounts have been established just for that reason. More extra twists have been put in the money flow to keep our transactions well disguised. We're now using accounts in the Cayman Islands and Switzerland in addition to those we've been using in the Channel Islands and the Isle of Man. We're also using even more features of the World Bank, the WTO, the IMF, and the International Acceptance Bank of New York."

Hugo pressed his lips together. "So you've made sure the money flow is as complex as possible?"

"It will never be as complex as possible, but I think it's complex enough," Wan replied. "You can always add more layers, but I can assure you we have everything more hidden than it was and it was okay before."

"Good," Hugo nodded slowly and gestured toward some more displays on the wall. "We'll move on to other things. As we've mentioned before, with all the capability we have here, we can choose between a huge assortment of methods to eliminate Baker and Gibson." He narrowed his eyes. "And I want to get them out of our way real soon. I think they're a gigantic pain in the ass."

"We've just received the two Poseidon Missiles from the Kremlin. They followed the delivery instructions perfectly and they're in the process of selecting some other types of missiles to send us," Oleg said. "We'll soon have even more options going forward."

Hugo rubbed his chin. "That's good. We have a

limited supply of the missiles we used the other day to bring down the German helicopters. If we can get some more soon they might be useful in eliminating all the people we need to get rid of." He scanned the faces around him. "We'll keep all of our options in mind as we go forward. We might move some missiles like we used on the helicopters over to the United States and put them in a good position. They have a limited range."

Oleg leaned forward. "We're still using Ludvig next, right?"

"Right," Hugo said. "I decided to allow him to do his face-to-face confrontation before we use snipers or missiles." He glanced at one of the displays on the large floor-to-ceiling circular screen and studied it for a few moments. He then pointed at it and looked at Oleg.

Oleg stared at the display and gave a thumbs-up.

"Gibson and Baker have a coordination meeting scheduled with the local law enforcement tomorrow at the Tuxtun offices. Will Ludvig be ready to do his part?" Hugo asked.

Oleg leaned forward. "Have you developed a plan yet for him to get through their security?"

Hugo made a sweeping gesture at the various displays on the screen. "With the power of our quantum computer, I'm sure we can work that out quickly." He looked at Oleg. "Tell him to get ready to do his thing tomorrow."

****

The next morning, Ludvig cautiously made his way forward in a large storage room inside the Tuxtun Headquarters Building. He walked toward a door that he knew opened into a hallway.

He patted the cell phone in his pocket. The software he had downloaded last night contained floor plans and the technology to unlock doors and make him invisible to all the security monitors. It was amazing, he thought. As long as he kept his cell phone in one of his pockets, the heat detection monitors, the motion detection monitors, and none of the other monitors would detect him. He was invisible to everything except human sight.

Ludvig stopped when he reached the door and studied the floor plan again. He had all the information he needed including the exact path and procedure he had used earlier to get on the premises.

When he was satisfied he had all the necessary details fixed in his mind, Ludvig stopped at the door and turned the knob. After he heard a click and opened the door, he moved into the hallway. It was comforting to know his cell phone was giving out signals to keep him invisible to all the security monitors. The capability Hugo and his group had provided to him was unbelievable.

Staying on full alert, Ludvig strolled down the wide hallway with his pistol in ready position. He could already see the room he was going to had an open door. He stopped just short of the opening and cautiously peeped inside the conference room.

No one was looking in his direction and he did a quick count. Eight people were sitting at the large table. Baker and Gibson were among them. They would die first and then the other six. In the past, he had eliminated more than that within just a few seconds.

Ludvig scanned the hallway again in both directions. It was still clear. He looked back into the conference room. Gibson was speaking. Everyone at the table in the room had their gaze fixed on him. Ludvig tightened his finger on the trigger of the silenced Heckler & Koch USP he carried in his right hand.

This was working out perfectly, he thought. He not only would eliminate Baker and Gibson, but he would also eliminate everyone in the room. That would be no extra trouble for someone with his skills.

The magazine in his pistol held 15 bullets. They were all 9x19 mm Parabellum cartridges. There were only eight people in the room, no problem. He had the right weapon, plenty of expertise, and plenty of ammunition.

He knew the sound suppressor on the end of his pistol wouldn't affect the impact of the bullets in any significant way.

As a safety valve, he always carried two additional magazines. He couldn't envision any way he would need them in this case but it was always smart to be prepared for unexpected problems.

Besides Baker and Gibson, he figured some of the other six people in the room could also turn out to be a problem for Hugo Wagner and his group in the long run. He was hired to resolve problems and he wanted to do an excellent job. It never hurt to enhance your reputation whenever you had a good chance to do it.

Ludvig scanned the hallway again.

Everything was still clear.

He prepared to make his move.

Chapter 9

"Things are constantly getting more complicated," Ralph said. "We need to do more research and get smarter too."

A sinister voice echoed from the doorway. "I agree you need to get smarter but none of you will get a chance to do that, too bad."

Vicious laughter ensued from the figure in the doorway.

When Ralph turned, his mouth dropped open.

Matt turned slightly and looked at the tall, muscular man who stood just inside the open doorway. The man's pistol was extended toward him.

The man was in a perfect position. Everyone was well covered.

"How did you get in here?" Ralph asked.

"Not difficult," the man said. He waved his pistol back and forth. "Don't try anything. These 9mm slugs carry quite an impact."

While keeping his pistol in the ready position and his finger tight on the trigger, the man removed a small sign from his jacket and placed it on the doorknob where it would be seen in the hall.

Matt could see the sign had red letters as the man quickly closed the door.

The man's gaze took in both Matt and Ralph. "The sign on the outside of the door says 'DO NOT

DISTURB.' No one is going to be coming in here."

"Who are you?" Matt asked.

The man grunted and then said, "I'm Ludvig Kats. Too bad you're not going to live long enough to get any benefit from knowing that."

Ralph's eyes narrowed. "So what do you want?"

"For all of you to die," Ludvig hissed. "You all have it coming. You've been in Hugo's way for too long."

"You'll die too. You can't evade everybody for very long," Ralph said. "Somebody in the CIA, FBI, or military will get you."

"Hugo and his group will deal with all of them later. I probably will too. I'll likely stay involved." Ludvig continued to laugh as he waved his gun back and forth at everyone sitting at the table. "Too bad none of you will live to see all of your pals in law enforcement destroyed." He laughed louder and seemed to enjoy the situation.

Matt noted Ludvig was obviously overconfident.

Thinking he could take advantage of that, Matt decided to try to get some useful information while he could. He slowly turned more toward Ludvig. "How did you get involved with Hugo?"

Ludvig gave a slight shrug. "I guess my boss told him I'm the best assassin on the planet."

"Who's your boss?" Matt asked.

Ludvig hesitated.

Since Ludvig was obviously Russian, Matt figured his boss was Oleg Titov, but he wanted to be sure.

"If we're all going to die we won't gain any advantage from knowing that," Matt said. He stared at Ludvig.

Ludvig seemed to agree and he quickly regained his bravado.

"And die you will," Ludvig said. He gave a big laugh. "Very soon you'll no longer be a big problem to Hugo and his group." He leaned toward Matt. "Okay, Oleg Titov is my immediate boss." He gave a slight shrug.

Steve pushed his chair in slow motion away from the table.

"Hold it right there." Ludvig pointed his Heckler & Koch USP at Steve. "That's far enough."

Steve froze.

Ludvig narrowed his eyes and stared at the group. "Don't try anything." He waved his pistol and looked at Matt. "I know all your tricks. I'm smarter than anyone in here." An evil grin radiated on his face. "I'm at least one step in front of all of you. I'll cut down the next one who makes any movement. And I mean any movement, no matter how small."

Matt could tell Ludvig was enjoying the situation immensely and might get a little careless. Matt remained prepared to take advantage of any opportunity that presented itself instantly. He had completed plenty of training to do that.

"Since we're all going to die anyway, would you tell us where Hugo is located in Germany?" Ben asked.

Ludvig laughed. "You're smarter than I thought. I'd tell you if I could, just to see your reaction." He shrugged. "The problem is, I don't know." He looked directly at Ben and laughed some more.

Without moving his head, Matt slowly scanned the room with his eyes. A plan was forming.

Ludvig extended his pistol toward Matt. His finger

tightened on the trigger. "Guess it's about time to go ahead and get this over with."

"One more question before we die," Matt said. He figured Ludvig was still enjoying the situation immensely and would allow a short delay in the action.

Ludvig eased the pressure from his finger on the trigger and waved his pistol back and forth among the people at the table. He continued laughing, obviously savoring every moment of enjoyment from his commanding position.

As Ludvig's laughter echoed through the room, Matt felt the plan forming in his mind would work. A wave of confidence flowed through him.

Ludvig continued to laugh as he leaned toward Matt. "So what's your question?"

"You're obviously a lot better than any of us. How did you develop all that talent you have?" Matt asked.

"I put in a lot of hard work." Ludvig shrugged and laughed again. "I got this assignment because I'm the best on the planet."

"How do you know you're the best on the planet?" Matt asked.

"Enough of your stupid questions," Ludvig said with a scowl. "It's time for you to die." He raised his pistol and pointed it at Matt. "It's time for you to say goodbye to everyone forever."

Steve turned his chair slightly and dove toward the floor under the table. His right hand grasped his Glock 19 and raised it to fire.

Ludvig fired first. A muffled pop sounded. The shot caused wooden splinters to explode from the top of the table, but Steve was still hit.

Steve dropped his pistol before he could get off a

shot, and slumped bleeding to the floor.

Before Ludvig could point his pistol back toward Matt, a loud bang sounded.

Ludvig's Heckler & Koch USP bounced on the carpet. He twisted, staggered forward, and dropped to the floor.

Several people at the table were now brandishing a weapon pointed toward Ludvig, but they hadn't been as quick as Matt.

Matt stood with his Glock 19 still pointed at Ludvig. The full metal jacket hollow point 9mm bullet had torn a hole in the left side of his chest, right where his heart was. Matt instantly knew Ludvig was dead and didn't fire again.

"He had it coming," Matt said as he turned toward Steve, who was groaning and stirring around on the floor.

Everyone converged on their injured friend.

Ralph fished a handkerchief out of his pocket and put it inside Steve's shirt where blood was oozing out, just below his right shoulder.

Ben leaned forward and inspected the wound. "Not too bad. Must have been a glancing blow."

"Yeah, it was, I was moving fast." Steve put his hand on the handkerchief and held it in place. "Hurts like hell," he said, as he struggled to his feet. "But I think I'm okay."

While placing his Glock back in the holster, Matt stared at Steve. "We'll get you to a doctor."

"No big rush," Steve said. He pulled the handkerchief back. "The blood flow's not real bad— bullet just grazed me. Hitting the edge of the table threw it off course just enough."

"Does your shoulder feel broken?" Matt asked.

Steve made a motion, something like a shrug. "I think it's intact." He forced a small grin. "I'm in charge of security around here. I felt like I needed to do something. I couldn't just sit there." He looked at Matt. "When you created the slight distraction by appealing to Ludvig's ego, I felt like it was time to act."

"You created the big distraction and gave me the opening I needed." Matt gave a thumbs-up. "You did your job as head of security."

Steve also gave a thumbs-up.

Ralph waved Steve toward the doorway. "Come on, I'll get someone to drive you to the emergency room. We'll have them take a look at your injury and make sure you get proper treatment. No need to take any chances on any complications, especially an infection."

****

At five o'clock p.m. local time in a mountainous region in southern Germany, Hugo Wagner, Oleg Titov, and Wan Lu sat at the doughnut-shaped round table in the middle of their hi-tech control room.

Hugo moved the red dot from his laser pointer to a display on one of the curved walls and stared at Oleg. "That didn't go well." He turned back toward the display and studied a close-up of Ludvig's motionless body being moved into an ambulance parked outside a side entrance into Tuxtun. "He's obviously dead. He has no hookup to any life-sustaining devices."

"Ludvig was our best assassin," Oleg said. "Something unexpected must have happened."

Hugo gave Oleg a long stare. "We can learn a lot of lessons from this. One is that we need to make better use of our technology. From this point forward, our assassins will use our new body-cams so we can see and hear everything that's going on in real time."

"We should have made that a rule earlier," Wan said. "We have the capability to closely follow every detail of every mission we assign."

Hugo grunted. "Yeah, we had a lot of other things we needed to do but we certainly should have taken time in this case to make use of our latest model body-cam." He regarded Oleg carefully. "I should have been more concerned about something going wrong but we provided Ludvig with hi-tech shielding so he could avoid being detected by their security system. We had also provided him with all the intelligence he needed to get into their building and maneuver to the right location." Hugo drummed his fingers on the table for a moment. "Also, I was relying on everything going right because of your assessment of Ludvig's superior capability."

"He was definitely our best. I would really like to know what happened," Oleg said.

Hugo exhaled sharply and leaned forward. "Well, this is all water under the bridge for now. Next time we'll use every hi-tech device we have to help us insure success and we'll have backup like I wanted to do in this case."

"And speaking of that," Wan said. "Our Chinese engineers have improved our surveillance capability. They've just developed a new hypersonic surveillance drone that can get better close-up images than any of our satellites."

"How much better?" Hugo asked.

Wan shrugged. "I don't have those details yet.

They're still testing, but I've been assured the images will be better and any noticeable improvement will help us in a lot of ways."

"The Americans will discover it," Oleg said. "They'll know what's going on and they might shoot it down."

"They won't be able to do that." Wan narrowed his eyes. "It travels at mach 5 and none of the American missiles can catch it."

"They'll figure out a way to intercept it," Oleg said.

"Why are you so negative about this?" Hugo asked.

"We keep underestimating the Americans and we keep losing," Oleg said.

Wan leaned forward. "Are you still upset about losing Ludvig?"

Oleg didn't answer.

A brief silence ensued.

Hugo looked at Wan. "How soon will one of these new surveillance drones be ready to use?"

"I've been assured we won't have to wait long," Wan said. "That's why I mentioned it."

Hugo turned back toward Oleg. "Wan is giving us some good news." Hugo smashed a fist on the table. "You need to get over losing Ludvig and get focused on moving forward. We have a lot of work in front of us."

Oleg nodded and made no comment.

A large smile dominated Wan's face. "We're going to like the additional capability we're getting." His gaze took in both Hugo and Oleg. "We can use the high-speed capability to get it to any area of our choosing quickly and then we can slow it down and stay in the area for a long time. When it needs to leave, it has the high-speed capability. And it has the best possible maneuverability. It can hover for long periods."

"What kind of fuel system does it use?" Hugo asked.

"This latest version is nuclear." Wan's smile broadened. "That gives it unlimited range and the ability to hover for an unlimited period."

Oleg laughed and gave a thumbs-up.

Hugo leaned forward. "That capability fits right into our plans. Going forward, we should know even more details about every aspect of our enemies before we choose to react." He started to say more just as his secure satellite phone rang.

Hugo glanced at the caller ID. "It's Jake Bolton. He probably found out some more about the Hidden Empire or he got another message from them."

"I hope they still approve of what we're doing," Wan said.

Hugo nodded as he pressed the button on his phone to answer.

Chapter 10

With the speaker function activated, Jake's deep voice resonated from Hugo's phone.

"I got another message from the Hidden Empire and they still generally approve of what we're doing, but specifically they want you to be careful in interfering with some of the world's monetary activities," Jake said.

"What's the problem?" Hugo asked.

"They know you're going to go after all the gold owned by the U.S. Mint and the Federal Reserve."

"How can they know that?"

"I have no idea but I guess they have their ways."

"Do you think they have the same capability we have, quantum computer and such?" Hugo asked.

"I'm not sure how they keep up with things but they seem to always know a lot about what goes on in the world, including what we're doing."

"Did the same person as the one last year get in touch with you?"

"I don't think so," Jake said. "Someone called me. They knew my private number. It was a male's voice, but I don't think it was the same person who called last time or the person who paid me a visit."

"So what do they want me to do, quit going after the gold?"

"You got it."

"Did he give you any reason?"

"Just that it would disrupt some necessary things involved in their money flow."

"Did he get any details?"

"Nope, that was the only explanation he gave."

"Did he say anything else?"

"He emphatically told me to contact you immediately and to let you know they would be watching everything you do."

"It would be great to know exactly who they are. Did you get any additional information about that?"

"No clues at all."

"Do you have any idea why they called you again instead of me?" Hugo asked. "They obviously have my number."

"When they called me last year, they knew I was the main person involved in setting up the operational framework for the revival of the Fourth Reich. I guess they wanted to make sure I was kept in the loop."

"The times we discussed this earlier you told me your information was too important and too sensitive to discuss in any way other than face-to-face. But this time you called on the phone. What changed?" Hugo asked.

"After I finished analyzing and investigating thousands of things to get you set up to launch the Fourth Reich, I improved the security on all of our phone systems. I figured it was now okay to use them to discuss all of our information, even if it's top secret information."

"When they called you this time, was there still no caller ID on your phone?"

"Still nothing and after he disconnected, I tried to trace the call using our latest technology. The call was untraceable."

Hugo raised an eyebrow and waited.

"The person who called emphasized they knew every detail about what we were doing and, like last year, he stated a few of our more significant activities in case I had any doubts."

Hugo narrowed his eyes. "And you're convinced they know every detail about what we're doing?"

"Yes," Jake said. "It would be very difficult for anyone to know any of the items he stated back to me. We're definitely dealing with a well-organized secret organization that has the ability to influence most, if not all, the significant events throughout the world."

"If I try to get in touch with them, I still have the phone number and the instructions you gave me before on how to make the call."

"The man who called me didn't mention that."

"I might try calling them again."

"That's your choice. Like I told you, the man didn't mention that."

"Okay," Hugo said. "You've delivered the message. Is there anything else you want to say before we disconnect?"

"Are you going to try to call them?"

"Of course."

"If someone answers, I'm curious about what you're going to tell them."

"I'm not sure," Hugo said. "I'll play it by ear. I, of course, want to find out more about them."

"If you can do that, it would probably help us in the future."

"My thinking exactly."

There was a brief silence.

"Before we end this conversation, do you have any more comments or anything else you want to discuss?" Hugo asked.

"Just one more comment, good luck."

"I can always use it." Hugo gave a short laugh. "Stay in touch and keep doing your normal work. I'll try to get in touch with them and I'll keep you posted."

"Thanks."

Hugo disconnected and scanned the faces around him. "Well, what do you think?"

"I didn't know you were still planning to take over the world's supply of gold," Oleg said.

"It's always been part of my plan." Hugo shrugged. "I haven't given up on it. It's an important part of being in control of the world."

"Have you done something lately to catch the attention of the Hidden Empire?" Wan asked.

Hugo made a sweeping motion with his right arm. "I've used all this capability to continue my research on the gold storage. Somehow they picked up on it."

"They must have equal capability, or maybe even better," Wan said.

Oleg nodded slowly and then looked at Hugo. "So they want us to continue our disruption of world activities but they don't want us to control the gold supply."

"That makes sense," Hugo said. "The Hidden Empire wants to maintain their control over things and they like the disruption we're causing, but they don't want to allow us to get too powerful." He gave a slight grin. "I guess we're supported as long as we stay within our boundaries."

"I think some people in the Kremlin who run the

KGB are part of this Hidden Empire," Oleg said. "I just get some hints now and then. I know some people in the Kremlin are part of the Illuminati. And I think the Illuminati are the same as this Hidden Empire, or they're at least part of it."

Hugo again made a sweeping motion with his right arm. "With all this capability, we can find out who they are as soon as we decide to spend time doing that."

Oleg and Wan both nodded.

"Well, let's see if I can talk to some of them in the Hidden Empire," Hugo said. He retrieved the number and instructions from a storage area in the computer system.

Hugo punched in the number on his phone. He noted the instructions stated he would hear three rings and then a dial tone like he had been disconnected but to stay on the line and not hang up.

After hearing the three rings Hugo heard that dial tone. He stayed on the line.

Within seconds, he got a message saying the number had been disconnected. Instantly, he heard another dial tone.

Hugo disconnected and looked at his partners. "That number is no longer in service."

"Makes sense," Wan said. "They apparently don't like to leave any loose ends around."

Hugo nodded slowly just as his phone rang.

There was no caller ID, but he knew who it was.

Hugo made sure his phone was on speaker before answering.

"State your name," the man said.

"I'm Hugo Wagner."

"Why were you calling?"

"One time earlier I was asked to call the number I punched in and I wanted to talk again," Hugo replied.

"What do you want to talk about this time?"

"One of my employees was contacted by someone in your organization to deliver a message to me. The message was to discontinue my activities immediately in order to increase my gold supply."

There was a long silence.

Hugo didn't disconnect. There was no dial tone so he figured he was still connected.

Hugo continued to stay on the line. In less than a minute, he heard a different male voice.

"My organization knows everything you're doing," the man said. "We'll always let you know if you're out of bounds."

"What's your organization, and who are you?"

"You already know we don't answer those types of questions. You now should know for sure we exist and you also should know for sure we're watching you."

Hugo waited and didn't comment.

"You can continue to pursue your objective to gain control of the world because we don't think there's any way you'll succeed and we like the disruption you cause," the man said, "but we won't allow you to do something that causes us a problem."

"How will my capturing the gold supply cause you a problem?"

There was another silence.

During this pause, Hugo figured there was a discussion going on about how much information to reveal. He waited for some type of response.

In a few minutes, someone at the other end of the call spoke into the phone.

"We won't give you any details," the man said, "but having the gold stored in its regular places allows us to use it to influence powerful people around the world."

"How do you use it?"

"I told you we won't give you any details."

"Is there any deal I can work out with you so I can at least get some of the gold?"

"No. It's important that the perceived safety of the gold storage areas not be compromised."

Hugo rubbed his chin for a moment and then asked, "You told me before that it's important for us to communicate. Is there any number you can give me that I can use to call you whenever I have a question?"

"If you have an urgent need to talk to us just call the same number you've been calling. We'll know it's you. It's not really disconnected. The way we have it configured now is just an added safety valve. We'll call you back."

"Okay."

"Remember, we're very well organized and powerful. We're watching every move you make as we allow you to go forward with many of your plans," the man said. "We don't think there's any way you can succeed in taking over the world, so you're not a threat to us for trying. As we just did, we'll let you know if there's something specific that will cause us a problem."

"I understand," Hugo said.

"We like the fact that you'll create a lot of disruption in the world while you're trying to take it over. It helps us keep everything we're doing as secretive as we need to."

"I know to back off the gold but otherwise I can keep doing what I want to do unless I hear back from your organization, right?"

"That's correct," the man said. "I think we're synced up again."

Hugo heard the line go dead. He then scanned the surrounding faces glaring at him.

"Okay, it looks like we're back in sync with the Hidden Empire," Hugo said. "I guess since I had the phone on speaker all of you heard the conversation clearly, right?"

Everyone nodded.

"Are you really going to stop trying to get the gold?" Wan asked.

"I'll wait a while before I take any action, but eventually I'll go ahead with my planning on the best methods for getting the gold," Hugo said.

"How long are you going to wait?" Wan asked.

Hugo shrugged. "I'm not sure at this moment. We'll see how things develop."

Oleg frowned. "They found out before what you were planning. They'll know if you go back to it."

"Not necessarily," Hugo said. "Earlier, I printed a lot of relevant information on getting the gold. "I'll study it and use it to complete my planning and not conduct any more computer research relative to the gold."

There was a brief silence.

"So, bottom line, you're going to defy them and go after the gold anyway?" Wan asked.

"Like I indicated, I'll wait a while to make that final decision. For now, we'll work a lot harder to try to find out more about the Hidden Empire. With all of our capability, we should be able to make good progress." He shrugged. "Who knows, we might end up conquering them too. If we really want to rule the world we'll need to get them out of our way and I think we're capable of doing that. I'm sure they've never dealt with any organization as powerful as we are."

****

The next morning at the FBI headquarters in Jacksonville, Ben sat at the large table in the main conference room with seven other people. Ralph, Matt, Todd, Judy, and Steve were there from Tuxtun. Justin and Vince were also there.

"All of our intel agencies have been busy and we have a lot of new information to discuss," Ben said. "NSA has decrypted some more data during the last twenty-four hours from the intercepted calls. Another quantum computer was mentioned in one of the intercepted calls. It looks like it's going to be used by both Russia and China to move the money around on some new joint projects they're planning."

"Will it be located at one of their embassies in Havana?" Matt asked.

"There's no information on that yet," Ben said. "But there have been more attempts to hack into our Federal Reserve System. Since we also have quantum computers, we've been able to block them so far."

"Should we take more aggressive action?" Matt asked.

"I recommend collecting a little more intelligence before we take any aggressive action. We don't want to react prematurely and create any new problems for ourselves." Ben exhaled slowly. "We're in an odd position. We need to help the Federal Reserve on some matters, but we have to be leery of the owners, especially the descendants who are still carrying on the work of their fathers. We know for sure the families of many of the original owners are still in place and they're all very secretive."

There was a brief silence.

Judy leaned forward. "The funneling of big money through dummy corporations is something we need to do more research on. We know for sure that's what Hugo Wagner and his cohorts are doing. The Hidden Empire might also be doing that. I think we have two layers of powerful organizations to be concerned with."

"The Hidden Empire is apparently a little better than Hugo is at doing this," Matt said.

Judy nodded. "They've been at it longer than Hugo, and they've apparently learned all the tricks."

Todd leaned forward. "We know Hugo also uses the World Bank, the International Monetary Fund (IMF) and the World Trade Organization (WTO) to set up seemingly legitimate projects and then funnel the money involved through dummy corporations to certain individuals and organizations. Of course, these individuals and organizations support Hugo's goal to dominate the world."

"I think the Hidden Empire does something very similar, except they're better at it," Judy said. "I think they also use the Federal Reserve System and the International Acceptance Bank of New York. And they do everything better than Hugo does. Since one of the creators of the Federal Reserve also established the International Acceptance Bank of New York a few years later, it makes sense that the Hidden Empire would have a better command of the subtleties of all the money flow."

"So you're thinking the creators of the Federal Reserve were also members of the Hidden Empire?" Ralph asked.

Judy nodded. "And the descendants of the creators of the Federal Reserve are involved in keeping it all going. Both Hugo and the Hidden Empire have created a convoluted money trail almost impossible to follow. We need to come up with some better analysis methods to gain more insight into what's going on there."

Todd gave a short laugh. "And that's not going to be easy."

"Easy or not, we need to do it," Ben said.

"What steps are you thinking we'll take next?" Ralph asked.

"Due to the international aspects, the CIA will continue to help us," Ben said. "My boss in Washington is in the process of getting all the new aspects of that help organized. We'll decide on our next step to take in this situation here after we get some more information."

Looking directly at Ben, Matt asked, "What exactly do you want the CIA to do?"

Ben spent a long time explaining the details.

"And remember Carmen Vargas and Hector Medina each have been released from jail," Vince said. "We're probably going to be hearing from them real soon. I'm sure they have a huge grudge against us."

Ben nodded. "They're somewhere in Mexico, according to my latest information."

Matt gave Ben a long stare. "So what's the bottom line for us right now?"

Ben glanced at Todd and shrugged his shoulders in response. "This situation reminds me of some of the chess analogies you've made. What were those comments you used to make about the number of options for a next move in certain situations in a chess game?"

Todd leaned forward. "Hugo obviously has a complicated plan that's in motion and we know the Hidden Empire is involved in a lot of this in some way." He rubbed his chin. "Chess does indeed have a relationship with what we're dealing with and there's a good analogy here. After ten moves in chess, a tree diagram of options has around 170 million branches. That's a big reason why we haven't figured out all the details yet. Deciding on our next move isn't going to be easy."

"Yep, our latest intelligence reveals a convoluted mess in many ways," Ben said. "And CIA analysts are pretty sure Cuba's role in this will increase. We know Oleg Titov is working with them on missile placements."

"Are Hugo and Wan directly involved in that too?" Matt asked.

"Yes, they're working right along with Oleg," Ben said. "The CIA thinks the missiles are coming from Russia and China and are strategically placed by Hugo and his group."

"Do you think the CIA has all the specifics on that yet?" Matt asked.

Ben shook his head. "Looks like one hell of a mess at the moment. It'll take time to figure everything out. I'm sure they'll tell us all they know when they have a little more of it untangled."

"With Carmen Vargas and Hector Medina on the loose again, Hugo will probably be working with both

Mexico and Cuba right now," Steve said. "A lot more assassins will probably be in the picture and coming after us. Some big things are definitely in the mix."

Ben glanced at some notes and spoke slowly, "We have a lot of issues to deal with and we now know for sure some of those issues will be connected in some way to The Hidden Empire."

Steve gave a short grunt. "It looks like the Hidden Empire is probably going to stay in the picture as we go forward."

Ben held up a large picture. "This is a mystery object we discovered yesterday flying over Jekyll Island."

"Weird looking helicopter," Justin said.

"It's definitely not one of ours." Ben looked at the picture. "And notice it has a stealth design. Radar doesn't pick it up."

"Who spotted it?" Justin asked.

"NRO analysts discovered it while reviewing late-night satellite surveillance photos," Ben said. "We're damned lucky to know about it."

Matt reflected that the National Reconnaissance Office (NRO) in Chantilly, Virginia designed, built, and operated our reconnaissance satellites.

"Do we have any clues about what it's doing or where it's going?" Ralph asked.

"Lot of possibilities, but the CIA thinks it's Chinese," Ben said. "They're still trying to figure out how it got into our airspace without being detected. We have special radar that can detect most stealth designs."

China still wants to be the dominant world power and we're still in their way." Judy shrugged. "They want to bring us down any way they can. They've been as active in technology and finance as they have in many other things. They might be planning to support Hugo and use a fleet of them to transport gold bullion from the Mint and the Federal Reserve to some remote storage vaults. They might be testing the design and capability of the helicopters."

"The permutations and combinations are endless here," Todd said.

Ben grunted. "Yeah, and the chess analogy still fits. There are a lot of possibilities here for determining our most lethal threat. A lot of shadows are in the mix. Hugo and his group, Russia, and China have a common objective right now to bring us down. And we don't know yet but the Hidden Empire might also have that same goal."

"Do you think the Hidden Empire wants to get us out of their way?" Matt asked.

"That's certainly a possibility," Ben said.

Matt thought about the Illuminati, the Freemasons, the Knights Templar, and several other secret societies and wondered if they all still existed. If so, how unified and involved were they? Based on what the United States intelligence agencies had previously discovered, he figured the Russian KGB was the enforcement arm for whoever was currently leading this initiative for world power. The Russian KGB could also be the enforcement arm of the Hidden Empire.

"How are we going to get this all sorted out?" Steve asked.

"I think we need to keep doing a lot of things we've been doing," Ben said. "Among those things, of course, is continuing to improve our security." He looked at Judy and Todd. "And it's important we keep working on following the money."

Judy nodded. "Todd and I are continuing to work on that and we have discussions with experts in the FBI and CIA on a daily basis."

"Stay on it," Ben said. "That's an important part of unraveling this quagmire of threats we're facing."

Judy scanned the faces around the table. "We mentioned the hi-tech helicopters earlier and wondered if their purpose might be to transport gold from the Mint and the Federal Reserve at some future time. Todd and I will continue to look into all the concerns about our gold supply."

"Has anyone discussed our concerns about the gold with the Mint and the Federal Reserve?" Ralph asked.

"Not yet, to my knowledge," Judy said, "But I know some FBI and CIA agents are planning to do that real soon."

Matt knew the Director of the United States Mint was responsible for several bullion depositories. Fort Knox was the largest of the ones the Mint owned, but it wasn't the largest bullion depository in the United States. The Federal Reserve had a larger one. He realized the gold concerns could be a complex puzzle in multiple ways.

"There's a huge global money flow involved in what we're dealing with," Judy said. "And we think the Federal Reserve is used as a clearing house for transactions within the United States in many cases. We know there have been millions of transactions involving both the World Band and the Federal Reserve in the last two weeks. That makes it even more important that we visit this new international office in the Jacksonville area very soon." She narrowed her eyes. "It's not common knowledge, but the Russians are heavily embedded in the world banking system. They're very involved in the activities of the IMF and the World Bank."

Matt began to get a better grasp of just how complex this situation was. Hugo was backed by Russia and China and he had a direct link to each country through Oleg Titov and Wan FU.

"Russia is the largest foreign owner of the gold stored at the Federal Reserve Bank in New York and that has only recently become the case," Judy said.

"Where does China rank on that?" Ralph asked.

"Right now, China is second to Russia in this particular case," Judy said.

"That's not surprising," Ben said, "based on some things we've just learned, Russia needs as many ways as possible to shield their other monetary transactions. They're probably trying to mix them in with a lot of their gold transactions."

"Todd and I will urge the law enforcement team we're working with to take a closer look at that," Judy said, "but they might not be able to gain access to all the information."

Everyone nodded.

Ben shook his head slowly. "This has evolved into the most complicated and intertwined stuff I've ever been involved with. Like before, we're dealing with a tremendous number of different threats from multiple sources."

"I suggest we just concentrate on moving forward one step at a time," Justin said. "Let's concentrate on checking out that new international monetary office next and see if we can gather any useful knowledge."

Matt narrowed his eyes. "And we'd better be prepared for some big shocks as we find out more about what will be going on there."

Chapter 11

Hugo Wagner sat in one of the four chairs in the center portion of the control room in his hi-tech fortress.

Oleg and Wan occupied two of the other chairs.

Hugo placed the red dot from his laser pointer on the image showing the new office building in the Jacksonville area, built to facilitate closer coordination of all the international monetary institutions.

"With our superior spying technology, we know that office is going to get a visit from a group containing Baker and Gibson tomorrow." Hugo glanced at Oleg and Wan. "Any more thoughts about what we want to do to eliminate Baker and Gibson?"

"I still don't understand why you're willing to spend so much time and effort to get rid of them," Wan said. "We can pursue all our goals to conquer the world from over here without having to worry about their interference."

Hugo bristled. "They were the primary force in shutting down my operations in the United States earlier. I'm not going to let them get away with that." He slammed a fist on the table. "They're going to pay for that. No one pushes me around and lives to brag about it."

"Wan has a point," Oleg said. "We don't really have to go to all this trouble to eliminate them."

Hugo narrowed his eyes and pressed his lips together. "But they're about to give us trouble again. We need this new coordination office in Jacksonville to enhance our global monetary flow and they'll probably try to shut it down like they did before." He banged his fist on the table again as his gaze focused on his two partners. "There's no way in hell I'm going to let them do that. Am I making myself clear?"

Oleg and Wan each gave a quick nod and didn't comment.

After a long hesitation, Wan said, "With our capability, we shouldn't be having this much trouble getting rid of them. We have a lot of options. We need to pick one that will work this time."

Oleg leaned forward. "Using Ludvig was a good option. He got in the building okay, but for some reason, he didn't succeed. He might have been overconfident and gave Baker too much time to react."

Wan nodded. "Yeah, all the news reports gave Baker the credit for killing him. There was no deviation in any of the reports on that."

Hugo pressed his lips together. "Also, we know experts at the FBI are inspecting Ludvig's phone but no problem there. I've remotely erased all the content."

Wan and Oleg each gave a thumbs-up.

Oleg turned slightly toward Hugo. "We have a good supply of missiles, all types. Why don't we just launch one of our intercontinental ballistic missiles toward a site in Jacksonville? We could target the FBI Headquarters or Tuxtun at some time when they're all in there."

"I don't think that's a good thing to do," Hugo said. "I don't want to give the United States Military a damned good reason to come over here and work with the German Military to make sure we're destroyed."

Wan leaned forward. "You're right. They would have to assume we would do that again and they couldn't allow that to happen. They would have to destroy us as soon as they could and of course they would have the full support of the German Government and military."

"The German Military has increased their activity on their search for us due to our shooting down their helicopters," Oleg said.

"But they don't have the urgency they would have if we started shooting missiles at targets in the United States." Hugo turned fully toward Oleg. "The German Government would cooperate fully with the United States on a matter like you just mentioned. Just stop and think for a moment on how urgent the search for us would get. They would be convinced we would shoot missiles at German targets too."

Oleg shrugged. "I was just thinking of a sure way of getting rid of Baker and Gibson."

Hugo gave a short laugh. "You're right, it would be effective, but we'll continue to use more conventional means for now."

Oleg shrugged again.

"Okay, let's get back to our planning," Hugo said. "We know Baker and Gibson are going to be in the group going over the new building we established to support our international monetary flow. We have a lot of options on how to knock them off. Let's put some details together."

Wan nodded. "Our satellites are in place all over the world, and all of our other spying equipment is fully functional. We'll know immediately if anything changes and if we need to be in a big rush to eliminate some other immediate threat. We have over ten thousand programs running at the same time on the quantum computer. Each one searches for specific things we want to know and displays the images and information instantly. We know what's going on all over the world."

"We have the very best of German engineering, Russian engineering, and Chinese engineering," Hugo said. "With our intelligence and hi-tech capability, we're able to keep up with everything going on and we're going to be impossible to stop, even by the Hidden Empire."

Oleg leaned toward Hugo. "And speaking of having a lot of options, when are we going to give Carmen and Hector their next assignment?"

Wan looked at Hugo. "Yeah, surely there's some way they can be useful on something to help us out."

"We could give them an assignment for getting rid of Baker and Gibson and we can also put them in charge of getting the gold bullion." Hugo made a circular gesture at the information on display. "We can make sure they have all the necessary data and let them spend time on putting a comprehensive plan together. We have plenty of other important things to spend our time on."

"What's your general thinking now on how to get the gold bullion?" Wan asked.

"I'm still planning on using our hi-tech helicopters to transport the gold to a large vault we'll build here at our location." Hugo mashed a few buttons on his control device.

A wooded, mountainous area appeared on one of the displays.

Hugo focused the red dot from his laser pointer on the wooded area. "Here's where we'll build the vault. The roof of the structure will have several landing pads for helicopters. We'll build the structure with an overhang that looks like more forest from the air. When the helicopters arrive with their payload, the overhang will be pulled back long enough to allow them to land. Once the helicopters have landed, the overhang will reset immediately and the area will again be totally undetectable. When the helicopters get ready to leave, we'll go through the same process."

Hugo grinned.

Oleg and Wan each gave a thumbs-up.

"We'll put Carmen and Hector in charge of doing everything necessary to get the helicopters fully loaded with gold over in the United States," Hugo said.

"Do you think they're capable of handling that?" Wan asked.

"They're smart people. We knew that when we first hired them," Hugo said. "They became billionaires by setting up an ingenious drug smuggling operation and running it to perfection. And I think they probably learned a few lessons because of their recent experiences. I think they'll do just fine on this project."

"When are you going to notify them and get them started?" Oleg asked.

"Today, why wait?" Hugo shrugged.

"Are you going to brief them on the planning you're already done?" Wan asked.

Hugo nodded. "I'll make sure they have all the relevant information to start with and if anything changes, we can keep them informed."

"Are you going to make them aware the Hidden Empire isn't going to like what they're doing in regard to the gold?" Oleg asked.

Hugo grunted. "Maybe, we'll see how things go. This is complicated enough without my throwing in more things for them to keep in mind."

Wan leaned slightly toward Hugo. "Are you still planning to get the gold from the Federal Reserve Bank of New York?"

"Absolutely," Hugo said. "They have five thousand tons there, and it's the largest gold repository in the world. The Swiss don't report their gold stocks but I easily got that information. They're not as large."

"The vault is eighty feet below street level and sitting on bedrock." Wan shrugged. "I don't think anyone can break in without having some unbelievable technology that we don't yet have."

Hugo laughed and looked at Wan. "I'm working on that. Give me some time. I have some options you might not know about. From previous research, I know there is an abandoned tunnel in the area. It was originally constructed for the Hudson & Manhattan Railroad, but has been forgotten over time. The existence of the tunnel might make the vault more accessible."

Hugo spent the next hour going through more of the details he had compiled concerning the massive gold heist.

"I think that's going to be too complicated for Carmen and Hector to handle," Wan said.

Hugo pursed his lips. "I'll make sure they have all the information we just discussed and access to necessary aspects of our technology. We'll keep in close touch with them while any parts of the heists are in process. I've already told you I think they're smart enough to pull it off."

Wan gave a noncommittal shrug.

Hugo looked at Oleg.

"I think you have a good plan and I think it's better for us not to actually do the work after the warning from the Hidden Empire," Oleg said.

Hugo looked back at Wan.

Again, he gave a noncommittal shrug and remained silent.

"Getting back to Baker and Gibson visiting the new international monetary office," Hugo said, "I think it would be a good idea for Carmen and Hector to be useful immediately and provide some assassins to give the visitors the proper welcome." He laughed.

Wan nodded. "Now that's a good idea. I know they just finished reorganizing their operations and I'm sure they took a good long look at their current manpower. They probably have some new top-notch assassins who would be perfect for the job."

Oleg gave a thumbs-up.

Hugo picked up his phone and started punching in a number.

"So you think the connection will be secure enough to discuss this on the phone?" Wan asked.

"It should be," Hugo said. "We have the phone system for Carmen and Hector set up in Mexico with our best technology."

****

In his luxury mansion in Mexico City, Hector looked across the round conference table in his office at

Carmen. "Thanks for driving over. Hugo insisted our phone system was secure, but I don't want to trust it. Since Hugo warned us about the Hidden Empire's concerns, I think it's best we don't discuss our plans over the phone."

"Yeah, it's always safer to have important discussions face-to-face." Carmen narrowed his eyes and leaned toward Hector. "And speaking of that, have you had your house swept for bugs?"

"Yes, I have my security team do that four times a day."

"Great, I do the same thing." Carmen took a deep breath and exhaled slowly. "Well, let's get to the business at hand and decide how we're going to complete our next assignment."

"Transporting the gold or providing the assassins?"

"Since the visit to the international monetary office is coming up tomorrow, we'll work on providing the assassins now and get that out of the way before we start working on all the other stuff involved with transporting the gold."

"Do we need to do anything specific to avoid attracting any attention from law enforcement?"

"We'll discuss that later," Carmen said. "Let select the assassins now and get them started toward Jacksonville."

"Do you have some in mind?"

"Yes, I do. When I started thinking about it, the names Ricardo Sanchez and Carlos Torres jumped out at me immediately."

"Any particular reason?"

"You might not have known about the incident, but just the two of them eliminated twenty members of a rival cartel."

"Just one of them should be enough for tomorrow if we plan it right. Why do you want to want to take a chance on losing two of our best assassins?"

"Because Hugo insisted on it," Carmen said. "He wants to be extra sure Baker and Gibson are eliminated this time."

"Did Hugo have any specific suggestions on things to keep in mind as we plan to get them out of our way?"

Carmen gave a slight shrug. "He told me there was no need to make it complicated. Just put together a good plan to ambush them when they're inside the building and then get rid of the bodies so they just disappear. The people in the building will be paid off well and they'll deny ever seeing them."

"Surely there will be evidence of some kind that Ben Fulton and his group went there." Hector leaned forward. "There has to be."

Carmen pursed his lips and narrowed his eyes as he stared at Hector. "Hugo assured me he would take care of that aspect."

"How will he do that?"

Carmen shrugged. "I asked him that same question and he told me not to worry about it. He insisted we concentrate on getting the assassins in place over there before Baker and Gibson show up tomorrow."

Hector tilted his head slightly and didn't comment.

Carmen leaned forward. "Okay, let's make sure we get our assassins in position in time to do their job." He picked up his phone.

"Who are you calling first?"

"Ricardo. He and Carlos are usually together. It should be the only call I need to make. The last time I talked to him he was in Saint Augustine."

Carmen punched in the number.

Chapter 12

Ricardo looked at his ringing phone. He noted the Caller ID and answered.

"Are you still in Saint Augustine?" Carmen asked.

"Yeah, is that significant?"

"Is Carlos with you?"

"Yeah."

"Do either of you have anything big going on tomorrow?"

"Nothing other than we're planning to go back to Mexico."

"I have an assignment in Jacksonville for you before you come back down here."

"What type of assignment?"

Ricardo listened for a few minutes as Carmen gave some details.

"What time do we need to be up there?"

"Get there early in the morning and get everything set up. I'll let you know when Baker and Gibson are on their way."

Ricardo laughed. "And I'll call you when we finish the job."

"Good. I'll call in the morning and I'll look forward to hearing from you after you finish the job." Carmen disconnected.

Ricardo looked at Carlos and explained their assignment.

"Did Carmen give you any type of instructions?"

"Nope, he just emphasized we need to kill everyone in the group, especially Baker and Gibson."

"Did he tell you how many are coming?"

"He's not sure but thinks it will be at least five. He thinks he'll know for sure when he calls to tell us they're on their way."

"Does Carmen know the reason they're coming?"

"He told me Hugo mentioned it was a routine visit by the FBI to check out the facilities and the basic business functions."

"Like what all they're planning to do there and how they're going to go about it?"

Ricardo nodded. "In short, that's a good way to describe it."

"So they might want a tour of the place?"

"Carmen thinks that's a real high probability."

Giving a big grin, Carlos said, "We haven't used our M20 Super Bazooka lately." He stared at Ricardo. "I'm very skilled in using it."

Ricardo narrowed his eyes. "What do you have in mind?"

"They're probably going to be in a pretty tight group if they're trying to hear what the tour guide is telling them. A well-placed shot from the bazooka should take care of all of them instantly."

"The bazooka wasn't designed for use indoors."

Carlos shrugged. "That shouldn't be an absolute limitation. I'm an expert in using it. We can make sure we get in a position where we have plenty of room behind us to minimize any effect from the back-blast."

"What about the people giving the tour?" Ricardo asked. "We don't want to kill them along with all the group Baker and Gibson are in."

"We'll work out a plan with them where they get in a position where they can quickly duck behind cover and that will be our signal to fire."

"We could just use a couple of grenades to wipe them out," Ricardo said.

"The bazooka will be better. There's a delay in the explosion with the grenades and the shell from bazooka will explode instantly. Two pounds of RDX/TNT explosive will do the job much better."

"We'll need to be in good cover ourselves to be safely protected from the explosion."

"After we get there we'll look things over and pick a good spot. We'll coordinate everything with whoever is giving the tour and then we'll be all set."

A brief silence ensued.

Ricardo looked directly at Carlos. "What if they don't take a tour?"

Carlos shrugged. "We have our AK-74 rifles and we have our pistols. We'll get them no matter what they do."

Ricardo hesitated for a moment and then grinned. "You have a point."

****

The next morning in front of a four-story modern office building south of downtown Jacksonville, Matt, Ralph, Justin, Vince, and Ben got out of a parked SUV and walked to the front door. As expected, it was locked.

Ben rang the doorbell.

After a few minutes, the door opened. A tall thin man with thick glasses stared at them. Two large heavyset men stood behind him.

Matt knew the guards had weapons. He could see the bulges in their coats.

Ben, Justin, and Vince held out their badges.

"We're from the law enforcement in the area," Ben said. "You have foreign ownership and we want to do a routine inspection of your building for security reasons."

The tall thin man looked at the badges and didn't comment.

Both security guards seemed concerned, but they also remained silent and held their positions.

"We need to come in and take a look around," Ben said.

"Have you inspected any other buildings in this area?" the tall thin man with a foreign accent asked.

"Yes, and this is a standard procedure by the FBI," Ben said. "We want to be aware of your general purpose for being here and we also want to have a basic understanding of how you're set up to operate."

Matt noted the security guards looked more uncomfortable.

The tall thin man narrowed his eyes. "This is a private business and we process a lot of sensitive banking information. We don't allow public access, even from the FBI."

"This is a routine visit," Ben said. "If you don't allow us an opportunity to look around I'll get a search warrant and you'll be flooded with a large number of agents inspecting everything in detail."

The tall thin man pursed his lips and frowned. He narrowed his eyes but remained quiet.

"Are you going to allow us access or not?" Ben asked.

"Maybe," the tall thin man said. "I'm the building manager and I need to make a phone call first. I'll get back to you in a few minutes." He shut the door.

Matt heard the lock click. He glanced at Ben.

"Looks like he might have something to hide," Ben said. "His bosses should realize they have no choice. They'll probably tell him to stop all the activity and show us around."

Ralph glanced at his watch. "We'll likely wait a bit for them to get ready for us."

"That's for sure." Matt gave a short laugh.

Everyone spread out, their senses heightened as they remained vigilant for any signs of trouble.

Matt carried his Glock 19 in a holster toward the back of his right hip, hidden behind his coat.

Everyone in Ben's group continued to stay on high alert while they waited for the man to come back.

****

Close to one end of a long hallway on the first floor of the financial office building, Carlos knelt on one knee and positioned the bazooka on his right shoulder.

"What are you doing?" Ricardo asked. "We can't fire from here. We need to have better cover so we can wait until they're all out in the open before they see us."

"I know that. I'm just practicing getting in position quickly and getting ready to fire. Maybe we can have some furniture or something moved out here. We'll see what we can work out with the building manager." He glanced toward Ricardo.

Ricardo gave a slight shrug. "Guess it's worth a try."

"If we had gotten here when we had planned to," Carlos said, "we would have had plenty of time to check everything out and get the building manager's opinion about the best place to set up our position for the kill."

"Well we're here now and the building manager knows the goal we have. Too bad he had to go answer the front door before we could look around and agree on a specific plan."

Carlos rubbed his chin as he glanced down the hallway. "Surely he'll check back with us before he lets them in."

Ricardo nodded. "We were assured he knows what the stakes are."

Carlos and Ricardo stared straight down the long hallway and waited.

When the building manager came into view at the far end of the hallway, he walked straight toward them.

"I haven't let the visitors in yet. They're waiting outside. My security guards are still at the door just in case they try a forced entry."

Ricardo and Carlos each gave a slight nod and made no comment.

"You getting here at about the same time they drove up and parked their car didn't give us any time to do that," the man said.

Carlos shrugged. "We were delayed by a traffic jam."

The building manager looked at the bazooka for a moment and then stared at Carlos. "Are you planning on firing that?"

"Once we have them in the right position," Carlos said.

"You can't use that in this facility," the man replied sharply.

"How many people are in the group outside?" Ricardo asked.

"Only five, and I was told you guys are experts with multiple weapons." The man pointed at the bazooka. "I don't understand why you need that."

Carlos grunted. "This bazooka is one of those multiple weapons you alluded to. We both have discussed this and think it will be the most effective way to kill a large group instantly."

"Five isn't a large group," the building manager said. "I was told you guys are among the best on the planet at using pistols. If you catch them by surprise you should be able to eliminate all of them quickly enough."

The man stared at both assassins for several seconds.

"You do want them eliminated, don't you?" Carlos asked.

The building manager shrugged. "I don't care. I never make those types of decisions. I just cooperate with my bosses when they ask me to do something."

"Are you going to take them on a tour?" Ricardo asked.

The building manager nodded. "That's what my bosses requested I do but they apparently weren't aware you were going to use a bazooka."

"Ricardo and I discussed this at length earlier," Carlos said. "That would kill all of them quickly and we will have completed our assignment so we can leave and get out of your way."

"I don't want to have an extended argument about that. My bosses made it clear they want them killed but I'm the building manager and I make the decisions about what goes on inside the building. You can use the bazooka outside, and that's final." The building manager stared at Ricardo and Carlos with a stern expression. He rubbed his chin for several seconds and gestured toward a side of the building. "There's a lot of cover outside over there and you shouldn't be noticed by anyone in the vicinity." He pointed at a door and looked directly at the two assassins. "Go outside where I'm indicating and wait at the front corner of the building. When you hear my signal, step around the corner and fire your bazooka."

"What's your signal?" Carlos asked.

"When they're leaving after the tour I'll let them get out to their SUV, which is about fifteen yards away from the front door and then I'll yell and say I have one more thing to show them. I'll wave some papers and wait for them to come back."

Both Ricardo and Carlos nodded and kept their gaze on the building manager.

"That will be your signal to step around the corner and fire."

"Do you have any way to ensure they'll be bunched up enough?" Ricardo asked.

"They all came in the same vehicle. They have to get close together to get back in it." The building manager gave a short laugh. "Since they will have just completed a tour of the building without incident, I doubt they'll feel an urgency to take a lot of precautionary measures when they turn back toward the building."

Ricardo and Carlos nodded as the building manager waved them toward the side door and then turned back toward the front of the building.

Chapter 13

Outside the front door, Ben and his group continued to stay spread out and on high alert.

Ben scanned the area as he turned slowly in a full circle. "That building manager is taking a long time."

"Might be planning how to knock us off," Justin said. "We'd better stay well spread out and on full alert."

Everyone nodded.

Ralph looked at Matt. "I'm glad we just completed the advanced course in our weapons training."

"Yeah, I was thinking the same thing," Matt said. "Being able to draw and fire in less than a second could come in real handy in any situation."

Ben walked over a little closer to Matt and Ralph. "I've just finished comparing notes with Justin and Vince. We all think this is shaping up to be a trap. We might be smart to call this off and go back to our offices. I can send some storm troopers back in full assault gear to check things out."

Matt glanced up at the sky and then scanned the tops of the building. "I've been staying on full alert like everyone else. Between the five of us, I think we'll immediately spot any sign of danger."

"There could always be something we haven't thought of and we end up not acting quickly enough," Ben said. "I vote that we leave now and go to my office. We can compare notes and decide what to do next. I'm probably going to favor sending in the storm troopers."

While everyone continued scanning the area, Matt took a quick glance at Ben.

"I don't really argue with your thinking but I'm willing to give it a few more minutes." Matt glanced at his watch. "Five more minutes to be exact. That will mean we will have waited here for thirty minutes. That's plenty of time for the building manager to reasonably discuss whatever he needed to with his bosses and get any directions from them."

Ben nodded and glanced at the other three men around him. "Any objections?"

Everyone gave a thumbs-up.

"Okay, we'll stay on full alert and give it another five minutes," Ben said.

Everyone continued to be on high alert, scanning their surroundings.

Matt saw movement out of the corner of his right eye. He turned toward the front door of the building.

The manager was motioning for them to come in.

Matt glanced at Ben.

"Stay alert and don't get too close together before we get in the building," Ben said. "Our mission is to inspect the business activity and it will be good to go ahead and complete it. Let's give it a try."

Everyone cautiously approached the front door.

****

The building manager stood in the open doorway at the front entrance and continued to motion for them to come inside.

They stayed spread out and approached the door in

single file. Ben was in the lead.

The two security guards stood slightly to one side and made room for the group to walk past them.

The building manager led them through a small lobby and into a long hallway. With the security guards following, he then ushered them into a large, empty room with multiple desks.

Matt guessed they didn't want his group to see all the nationalities that might be involved. He noted a large screen and a keyboard were on each desk. Were all the screens and keyboards connected to a large remote central computer?

"Do you normally have a lot of people in here?" Ben asked.

The building manager shrugged. "We have some people who come in on occasion and help us with some things."

"What types of things?" Matt asked.

"They help us with certain international banking issues during peak hours," the building manager said. "We want all the necessary transactions to get through on a timely basis. The main reason for this office is just to provide more oversight for our global financial systems and more service to resolve any unexpected issues."

"Global systems such as used by the World Bank, the WTO, and the IMF?" Matt asked.

The building manager narrowed his eyes and didn't comment.

"You provide service to them, don't you?" Matt asked.

Both security guards frowned and glanced at the building manager. They seemed ready to draw their weapons.

Matt and Ralph had practiced for this situation multiple times. Matt knew each of them could have his pistol in firing position in less than a second if necessary. He figured Ben, Justin, and Vince would react quickly too.

The building manager shrugged. "We're here to improve the service to many banking entities. The ones you mentioned are some of our customers. The Federal Reserve and the International Bank of Acceptance in New York are also some of our customers. That's a big reason we need an office here in the United States."

Matt turned slightly and gestured toward the equipment on the desks. "Is all this connected to a large computer?"

"Of course, we can't do our job if we're not online to a superfast computer that's connected to a superfast network." The building manager gave a short laugh and then waved them back into the hall.

As expected, the security guards continued to follow the group. Matt always kept them in his line of sight. He knew the others in his group were doing that too.

The building manager walked down the hall and pointed to a lot of individual offices and several large conference rooms. No one was in any of the offices or conference rooms.

The building manager waved the group forward and they went in and out of two more rooms with a lot of desks, screens, and keyboards identical to the first room they had visited.

The building manager turned and started walking back up the hall toward the lobby. He looked at the visiting group. "That concludes the tour. Is there anything else you need to do at this time?"

"That's all we need for now," Ben said. "Thanks for the tour."

Without saying a word, the building manager nodded and led the way through the lobby.

When they got back to the front entrance, the building manager opened the door and gestured toward the outside. "We're hoping we can perform an important international function without being harassed constantly," he said, "but we'll continue to be as cooperative as is reasonable."

Matt thought the building manager looked a little irritated as they all filed past him and out toward the SUV.

****

When the visiting group all moved outside and walked toward the SUV, Ben said, "Well that went smoothly enough, but stay alert while we get back into the SUV."

Matt glanced back at the front door. It was closed and there was no sign anyone inside the building was watching them.

Ben glanced back at the front door too and then looked at Matt. "It doesn't look like anyone is watching us right at the moment. If you run back quickly and position yourself up against the front wall between the door and one corner, you can provide some extra security for the four of us while we get in the SUV. I'll start it quickly and you can run and jump in if nothing happens."

"Are you going to check the SUV for any explosives that might have been planted while we were on the tour?" Matt asked.

"Definitely, and that will take a few minutes," Ben said. "That's another reason for having you keep a lookout until the rest of us are in the vehicle and ready to leave."

Matt nodded and ran back toward the building.

Ben and the other three spread out a little more and continued toward their parked vehicle.

A few moments later, Matt saw Ben and his group arrive at the SUV and then engage in a short discussion.

Ben got in the vehicle and shortly the four of them had the hood raised and were doing a detailed inspection.

Within another few seconds, Matt saw the front entrance door swing open to his right.

The building manager walked out a few feet and yelled, "Hey, don't leave yet. I have a brochure I want to give you." He raised his right arm and frantically waved something he had in his hand.

While Matt was looking at the building manager he heard a noise to his left.

Two men came around the corner holding a bazooka aimed at the group surrounding the SUV.

Matt could see they hadn't noticed his presence.

One of the men squatted and raised the bazooka to his shoulder.

In the next second, Matt fired twice before they had a chance to fire the weapon. Both men dropped to the ground.

Matt whirled back to his right.

The two heavyset security guards were charging toward him and were in the process of drawing their pistols.

Matt fired two more times.

Both men dropped.

All four men at the SUV drew their pistols and charged back toward the building.

The building manager stood at the front door with both hands in the air. Ben and the two police chiefs quickly surrounded him.

Ben, Justin, and Vince each made a quick call.

In less than fifteen minutes, the place was swarming with policemen and FBI agents.

Four ambulances arrived.

Ben had a brief discussion with some of the new arrivals and then looked at the group with him. "There's nothing more we need to do here. Let's get back to the FBI building and evaluate the situation."

Chapter 14

In his hi-tech fortress in southern Germany, Hugo Wagner sat in one of the four chairs in the center portion of the control room.

Oleg and Wan were present as well.

Hugo placed the red dot from his laser pointer on the image showing the new office building in the Jacksonville area that had been built to facilitate closer coordination of all the international monetary institutions.

"Well, our planned financial operation in Jacksonville has just come to a dismal end," Hugo said. He pressed his lips tight and stared at Oleg.

"Carmen and Hector never mentioned the possibility their assassins might use a bazooka," Oleg said. "If they had, I certainly would have been against it."

Wan turned his palms up and spread his arms. "That was a crazy thing to do."

Hugo reached for his phone and punched some digits. He heard Carmen answer.

"Why in the hell were your assassins using a bazooka?" Hugo asked.

"Did it work?"

"Hell no. We just watched all the action outside of the building. They never got a chance to fire it!"

" Your guys blew it big time."

Carmen remained silent.

Hugo disconnected and glanced at Oleg and Wan. "Well, we need to decide what we want to do next. We still have plenty of capability without having that office in the United States."

"Yeah," Wan said. "I don't think we should overreact. All of our satellites are in place all over the world and all of our other spying equipment is fully functional." He looked directly at Hugo. "We can still put a good plan together to eliminate Baker and Gibson."

Hugo leaned forward. "We just saw Matt Baker in action. Like we already knew, he's pretty damned good."

"Ludvig wasn't the only great assassin I had," Oleg said. "Roman Zak is available for an assignment. We could use him and this time we'll make sure he wears one of our hi-tech body cams."

"We've already used a Russian assassin and two Hispanic assassins." Wan's gaze took in both Hugo and Oleg. "All have failed to eliminate Baker and Gibson."

"So, do you want to use one of your Chinese assassins?" Hugo asked.

"I have two of them ready to go," Wan said. "Each is solid muscle and capable of killing people with their bare hands, if the need arises." Wan gave a slight shrug.

"I also have a couple of German assassins who're available," Hugo said. "Each one is good with pistols and rifles and are excellent snipers. We'll have a little more discussion and then pick our next option."

"We should have no trouble gathering the necessary intelligence to do our planning," Wan said.

Hugo laughed. "With our intelligence and hi-tech

capability we're going to know everything that directly relates to our next mission and I still think we're going to be impossible to stop in the long run." He tightened his lips and stared at both Oleg and Wan. "We should be able to eliminate Baker and Gibson easily without using a missile. Let's come up with another plan and get it done this time."

Oleg and Wan nodded.

Hugo looked back at the displays on the wall and then spoke some instructions to the artificial intelligence in control of his software setup. The displays on the wall changed.

After focusing his laser pointer on a new display, Hugo began talking.

The discussion lasted for two hours.

When it concluded, Hugo exhaled slowly and leaned forward. He regarded Oleg and Wan carefully. "Well, I think we've analyzed this from just about every possible angle."

Oleg grinned. "It's like our chess masters do in a chess match."

"Yep," Hugo said. "Chess definitely has a relationship to this. It's tied to game theory." He rubbed his chin. "I think we have a really good plan and this time we should succeed."

Oleg and Wan each gave a thumbs-up.

****

In an elaborate castle in Switzerland, Vulcan, Neptune, and Apollo sat in a plush lounge area and began their next meeting.

"Thanks for getting here promptly," Vulcan said. He leaned forward. "I received some more information from Thor."

Vulcan started to say more when a loud clap of thunder shook the building.

"I guess it's appropriate you've been communicating with Thor," Apollo said. "The God of Thunder is certainly a relevant entity in this situation."

Everyone laughed.

"Well, I think Thor being involved in this is appropriate for another reason." Vulcan took a long puff from his pipe and scanned the two faces around him. "I've already mentioned his bosses are deciding on what measures to take against Hugo and he's expecting them to communicate with him soon about what they decide."

"Do you think they'll decide to eliminate Hugo?" Neptune asked.

"Maybe," Vulcan said. "Thor mentioned they'll first give him a chance to modify his world conquest strategy and not interfere with the global money flow. It seems Hugo is still planning to empty all the gold from three Mint locations and the Federal Reserve Bank of New York."

"So he's still going after the Mint gold depositories in Denver and West Point in addition to Fort Knox?" Apollo asked.

Vulcan nodded.

"Counting the gold in the Federal Reserve," Apollo said, "Hugo could control tons of gold if he goes ahead with his plan and succeeds."

Vulcan nodded and rubbed his chin. "And if he takes that much gold out of the global monetary system it would certainly change things for us. We can't allow him to do that."

Apollo and Neptune both frowned and waited for

Vulcan to continue.

"The changes would affect us in a very negative way," Vulcan said. "We couldn't continue to operate the way we do now."

"Did Thor mention how soon our bosses are going to communicate with Hugo about that?" Apollo asked.

"Our bosses have already communicated with him twice about the gold," Vulcan said. "And Thor made it clear we'll give him one more chance to change his plans or he'll have to be destroyed."

"Hugo has a very secure setup. He might have the best technology on the planet." Neptune leaned forward. "We must consider the possibility we might not be able to stop him."

"We know where he is and we have a lot of options," Vulcan said. "We can wipe him off the face of the earth if we choose to. He might not realize we're that powerful."

"The United States Government and the German Government are looking for him and they haven't yet found his location. Are you sure we know where he is?" Apollo asked.

"Yes, we certainly know where he is and we'll destroy him if he doesn't change his plans," Vulcan said. "Thor told me our messenger will deliver a stronger message to him. Our messenger will make it very clear that Hugo and his entire group will be eliminated if he doesn't cooperate."

****

The next morning in Jacksonville, Ben sat at the large table in the main conference room at the FBI headquarters. Seven other people were around him at the table.

Matt, Ralph, Judy, Todd, and Steve were there from Tuxtun. Justin and Vince were also there.

Six large monitors were on the walls. Each displayed a lot of information containing both text and images.

Ben made a sweeping motion with his right hand toward the walls. "We have a lot to discuss."

"Hope this new information clears some things up and helps us make more sense out of what's going on," Matt said.

Ben shook his head slowly. "I think it goes the other way." He leaned back in his chair. "In my opinion, it confuses things further. That is, unless some of you can make more sense out of all this than I can."

There was a brief silence as everyone studied the information on the six displays and waited for Ben to continue.

"NSA detected a wire transfer for ten million dollars from the IMF to a bank in the Channel Islands. The CIA financial experts have investigated and they don't know who established the account but they know a person named Jake Bolton has access to it," Ben said.

"Who's Jake Bolton?" Matt asked.

"A lot of people are checking on that as we speak," Ben said. "I'll get back to that later." His gaze focused on Matt. "Those funds were earmarked for a private sector project with the IFC."

Matt knew the IFC was the International Finance Corporation of the World Bank Group, which was usually referenced as WBG.

"Is there another component of the WBG involved in the transactions?" Matt asked.

Ben focused the laser pointer on one of the displays

on the wall. "It looks like the IBRD, the International Bank for Reconstruction and Development, is also involved."

"One of the five sisters," Judy said. "I've done a lot of research on them. The WBG is actually a family of five international organizations responsible for providing financial benefits and advice to countries for economic development and eliminating poverty. A few insiders can throw a good smoke screen over selected financing."

Ralph turned slightly toward Judy. "Would you refresh my memory on the five sisters?"

"They're referred to as agencies, IBRD, IDA, IFC, MIGA, and ICSID," Judy said.

Ralph narrowed his eyes and started to ask another question.

Ben raised a hand. "Judy will explain all that to us later. Let's concentrate on figuring out some other things, including who Jake Bolton is."

"I assume the IMF, IFC, and IBRD won't voluntarily furnish any information about the wire, right?" Matt asked with a thin smile, figuring this was a no-brainer.

"Of course they won't," Ben said.

"Do your experts have any guesses as to what the ten million is for?" Ralph asked.

"Not yet but I'm hoping to get specific information or at least get some good guesses when our analysts furnish their report," Ben said.

After taking a deep breath, Matt mulled over the situation. Jake Bolton had just received ten million American dollars, probably for some kind of service. What was the service? Who was he working for?

Where was he located? Matt shook his head and stared at the ceiling.

"Interesting puzzle, huh?" Ben scanned the faces around the table.

Everyone nodded but no one commented.

Ben hesitated a moment and then said, "I have a few thoughts to run by all of you. I'm interested in hearing your comments."

Matt narrowed his eyes as he waited for Ben to continue. He was curious as to which direction Ben was going to steer them. There were an overwhelming number of things to think about.

"There are some likely threats to our immediate area we need to prepare for and even some remote ones like Hugo Wagner targeting the Kennedy Space Flight Center with a missile," Ben said.

"Do we have any evidence of that?" Matt asked.

"The Russians know we still have a Star Wars program there and we know they want to eliminate it. Hugo knows that too and he has the same reasons as the Russians to eliminate it. The Director of National Intelligence continues to warn me about that," Ben said.

Matt knew the Director of National Intelligence served as the head of the sixteen-member United States intelligence community; the FBI and CIA were two of the sixteen organizations.

"Every agency has contributed some useful information in the last few weeks," Ben said. "We know Oleg Titov is part of Hugo Wagner's team and might urge him to take action in that regard."

Ralph leaned forward. "The Kremlin might do that directly. They have the capability and the motivation. They don't need Hugo Wagner's help."

"The consensus from our intelligence community is that they would prefer Hugo take care of that," Ben said. "The Kremlin doesn't want to start World War III by being directly involved."

"Why do we need to be involved in this particular aspect of the overall situation?" Todd asked.

"All of us in this room know a lot about Hugo Wagner and his partners and we're accustomed to dealing with them," Ben said. "We're also close to the Kennedy Space Flight Center. Washington wants us to go take a look at things down there and be ready to provide some advice if needed."

"The Star Wars initiative continues to be privileged information, I assume?" Matt stared at Ben.

Ben nodded. "Some of it can be disclosed in certain circumstances."

"Which ones?" Ralph asked.

"I think this could be one of them." Ben leaned toward Ralph and Matt. "It could be Hugo Wagner might be planning to deliver that particular initiative a knockout blow." He gave a slight shrug. "Anyway, that's my guess."

"Can you tell us if the Star Wars objective is still the same?" Matt asked.

"Yeah, you need to know that." Ben rubbed his chin for a moment. "We know they're still planning to launch that powerful new laser down there. It's labeled as some kind of blaster."

"When's the launch?" Ralph asked.

"Don't know. The whole thing continues to be very secretive," Ben said, "even to me."

Ralph frowned. "Bet the press picks up on it."

"The Russians seem to know." Ben took a deep

breath and exhaled sharply. "Probably those damned moles."

"A nuclear explosion in the area would certainly put an end to the activity there," Matt said.

Ben looked at Matt. "Yeah, we'll probably be part of some discussions real soon on the best way to protect them and we need to be more knowledgeable. We'll visit the Kennedy Space Flight Center tomorrow morning. You and Ralph will go with me. We'll fly down there in our FBI plane. I've already obtained the necessary clearances."

Chapter 15

The next morning at Cape Canaveral in Florida, Ben, Matt, and Ralph were escorted into a building at the Kennedy Space Center on Merritt Island.

Soon, they were sitting in a large control room in Launch Complex 39 and listening to the first of a series of briefings.

After the third person finished his lecture, a tall man with a mustache entered the room. He introduced himself as Charles.

"What do you think about the overall setup?" Charles asked.

"There's a lot more to it than we thought," Ben said.

"Launch Complex 39 isn't the only place for launch operations at Kennedy Space Center on Merritt Island." Charles gave a slight smile. "Other launch operations take place next door at CCAFS. That's Cape Canaveral Air Force Station."

"Is CCAFS part of Patrick Air Force Base?" Ralph asked.

"It's a detachment of the 45th Space Wing of Patrick Air Force Base," Charles said. "We have quite a few active launch pads that most people don't know about. We've built forty-seven launch complexes since 1950. Many are still active in spite of discontinuing the space shuttles."

"Are we going to visit Patrick today?" Ben asked.

"Maybe," Charles said. "We're just hitting the high points, but we still have a lot to cover." He hesitated a moment. "We'll have lunch and then see how our time goes."

"We need to see everything to get a proper feel for the best way to assist you," Ben said, "assuming there are any problems that require the FBI's help."

Charles nodded. "That's why we're providing this information session."

"Judging from what we've already seen, CCAFS has its own separate airfield." Matt gave Charles a long stare.

"That's the Cape Canaveral AFS Skid Strip," Charles said. "It has ten thousand feet of runway that's convenient for delivery of large payloads for the shuttles and satellites. It's just a short hop from the runway to here, or to any of our launch sites." He narrowed his eyes. "We need to protect this whole area and we have a lot of security in place. At the moment, we think we have everything well secured." He looked at his guests. "We have parts of the Star Wars Initiative going on in various buildings throughout the island. We're spread all over the place and we try to keep it all secret to the public."

"Do you have anything specific in mind the FBI could help with?" Ben asked.

Charles shook his head. "Not at the moment. My boss assures me we're well secured. We did this as a courtesy. We try to cooperate with the FBI. It's a good policy since we might need your help later on some matters."

"Hugo Wagner, Russia, and China are all obviously

concerned about our missile defenses," Ben said. "They want their missiles to pose a big threat to us. It increases their world power."

"Of course, that's why we want an effective shield in place. It's a deterrent against an increase in their world power." Charles smiled. "We also have activity on some elements of the Star Wars Program at Goddard Space Center in Green Belt, Maryland, and Wallops Flight Facility on Wallops Island, Virginia." He looked directly at Ben. "The military is providing most of our security right now but you and the CIA could get involved sometime later, if needed."

Ben nodded. "There should be something specific the FBI could do to help you right here in this area."

Charles flashed another smile. "You're already helping. We know you're watching our backs and trying to deter Hugo Wagner. That's why my boss wanted you to be more aware of what we're doing. And I think we now have you thoroughly briefed."

Ben and his group left a short while later to go back to Jacksonville.

While approaching the plane, Matt said, "Guess we can't complain about being bored."

Everyone laughed. It was good to not let the tension build up.

****

In his hi-tech fortress in southern Germany, Hugo Wagner sat in one of the four chairs in the center portion of the control room.

Oleg and Wan sat in two of the other chairs.

Jake Bolton sat in the fourth chair.

Hugo turned toward Jake and made a sweeping motion with his right hand toward the images and data on the multiple displays around the room. "You can see how much data we have on display right this moment. We can instantly have millions more pieces of information if we can come up with any specifics on what we're looking for."

"Everything was the same as last time except a different man came to see me," Jake said.

"That was the only thing different?" Hugo narrowed his eyes and regarded Jake carefully.

Jake nodded. "I paid close attention to everything."

Hugo frowned and looked at Jake. "No clue about where he came from or what nationality he was?"

Jake shook his head and blurted out, "Absolutely nothing. He was white with no distinguishing features and he spoke English like the other guy. Neither had any accent."

Hugo grunted. "None of the people I've spoken to on the phone had an accent either." He shrugged and stared at Jake. "Well, what did he tell you this time?"

"He told me to let you know that you're absolutely forbidden to go after the gold or to shoot a missile into the United States. He emphasized neither of those things will be tolerated."

"Did he say what the consequences were?" Hugo asked.

"The messenger told me they know your exact location and they'll completely destroy you if you don't comply."

Hugo laughed.

"What's funny?" Oleg asked.

"They're bluffing," Hugo said. "No one knows where we are. All the resources of the German Government and the United States Government have been trying to find us for months. They can't do it and neither can anyone else, including the Hidden Empire. Our billions of dollars have provided superior technology that works in many ways to shield us from any possible detection. No matter how hard they try, no one will ever find us."

Hugo looked at Jake and again made a sweeping gesture at all the displays around the room. "We need to find out more about this Hidden Empire. Is there anything you want to discuss or do you have any suggestions about any specific information to look up?"

Jake slowly scanned the displays. "I don't see anything I think I need to discuss at the moment. I think the three of you will be the best ones to dig up and examine any clues relating to the Hidden Empire."

Wan leaned toward Jake. "We have hundreds of analysts available to help us examine things but, since you've met a couple of them, you're still very important in helping to uncover clues about them. Stay alert and keep us informed."

Jake nodded.

Wan studied Hugo for several moments. "So you're going to continue to go after the gold and you'll destroy places in the United States with missiles when you choose to?"

"You got it." Hugo laughed again, louder this time. "No one is as powerful as we are. We need to keep that in mind. We don't have to back down from anybody."

"Maybe the Hidden Empire has powerful technology we don't know about," Wan said.

"That's not likely." Hugo tightened his lips for a moment. "I spent almost a trillion dollars on this setup and our combined engineering expertise is the best in the world. I think the Hidden Empire is bluffing. There's no way they can destroy us even if they, by some chance, are able to find out where we are. Our security cannot be penetrated, even if they shoot missiles at us. We have an anti-missile defense that can block any attack."

Oleg glanced at Wan and nodded slowly.

A brief silence ensued.

Hugo looked at Oleg and Wan. "Maybe one of you has something in mind to ask Jake. Surely there's some way we can start finding out more about this Hidden Empire."

"I have some comments before I start asking questions," Wan said. "English apparently is the language the Hidden Empire chose to use for their communications. That should give us a clue about their leadership. We need to keep that in mind." He looked at Hugo. "The fact that our group is from Germany, Russia, and China respectively should have prompted them to use some other language. I'm surprised they didn't speak to you in German when you were talking to them on the phone."

Hugo shrugged and didn't comment.

Wan looked at Jake. "Did the man who paid you a visit want Hugo to call them again?"

"He didn't say anything about that," Jake said. "He just kept emphasizing I needed to specifically warn Hugo about going after the gold and about making plans to hit the United States with a missile."

Wan nodded slowly and glanced at Oleg.

Oleg gave a slight shrug. "I think we've covered everything." He then looked at Hugo.

Hugo leaned toward Jake. "Do you have anything

else to say?"

"That's it for now," Jake said. "Like Oleg mentioned, we've covered everything and I've delivered the message."

"Okay, you did your job. We'll go through our normal exit procedure." Hugo pressed a button on his phone.

Someone quickly arrived to escort Jake out of the control room.

Hugo turned to the two men present. "Well, we need to decide what we want to do next. We have several priorities now. We still need to eliminate Baker and Gibson, we want to get the gold, we want to eliminate more obstacles to our world conquest, and we want to put more work into finding additional information about the Hidden Empire."

"Yes," Wan said. "As for Baker and Gibson, we still have plenty of good assassins available." He looked directly at Hugo. "I recommend we put another plan together right now to get them out of our way."

Oleg nodded as he leaned slightly toward Hugo. "Like I mentioned earlier, Ludvig wasn't the only great assassin I had. Roman Zak is just as skilled and he's still available for an assignment. We could use him and we'll make sure he wears one of our hi-tech body cams so we can monitor everything that goes on."

"And, remember, I have two Chinese assassins ready to go," Wan said.

Hugo grunted. "Yeah, yeah, you keep telling me that and I remember. This time, I'll be a little more conventional and use one of my German assassins." He looked back at the displays on the wall and then spoke some instructions to the artificial intelligence in control of his software setup.

The displays on the wall changed.

After focusing the laser pointer on a new display, Hugo began talking. The discussion lasted for thirty minutes.

"Well, I think we've analyzed this from just about every possible angle and we'll ambush Baker and Gibson separately at their homes tomorrow night in Jacksonville," Hugo said. "Roman Zak will ambush Baker. Jonas Schulz will ambush Gibson. Each assassin will wear a body cam. I think we have a really good plan and this time we should succeed."

Oleg and Wan both nodded.

****

The next morning at the FBI Headquarters in Jacksonville, Matt, Ralph, Justin, Vince, Judy, Todd, and Steve sat with Ben at the large table in the main conference room.

"I just received a lot more intelligence on Hugo Wagner and his group," Ben said. "I wanted to discuss it right away so everyone would be aware of the latest information."

"Have we found his location?" Justin asked.

"Not yet, but we have a lot of new data and some of it could turn out to be real valuable to know," Ben said. "We'll discuss it and try to put our added knowledge to good use."

Everyone remained silent while they waited for Ben to continue.

"There was more information about some assassins who're currently working for Wagner. Roman Zak and Jonas Schulz were both mentioned in some recent phone calls NSA intercepted," Ben said. "One of them is Russian and the other is German." He shrugged. "I guess that's pretty obvious from the names."

No one commented.

Ben leaned forward. "Roman Zak is a top expert with most weapons and a master of hand-to-hand combat, all forms. He has better fighting credentials than anyone I've ever known about." Ben's gaze took in both Ralph and Matt. "I hope neither of you has to cope with him."

Matt made no comment. Neither did Ralph.

"We need to decide what to concentrate on next. There are a lot of options," Ben said. "Don't want to give the enemy any extra lead time. Remember, we have at least one mole in Washington, maybe more."

Ralph and Matt each gave a slow nod.

"Are we going to play offense or defense?" Matt asked.

Ben shrugged. "That depends on how things develop. Naturally, I prefer to play offense. We'll discuss more of the current situation and then decide on what action to take next."

"Before we talk more about the assassins we have something else to discuss. We've received another request from Federal Reserve officials to come check some things," Ben said. "They're still concerned about computer hacking, especially from Hugo Wagner." He shrugged "It's unusual they keep asking for help. Until recently, they never wanted us to look into any of their affairs, but I think they're pretty stressed at the moment."

"They're obviously more concerned about Hugo Wagner than the chance we'll discover sensitive information about what's going on behind the scenes,"

Judy said.

"You're referring to all the conspiracy theories, right?" Ben asked.

Judy gave a slow nod.

Ben's gaze focused on Judy. "A lot of our experts are convinced something odd is going on at the Federal Reserve. We need to keep that in mind during any discussions with them."

Ralph narrowed his eyes. "Some of the stuff we've discussed among ourselves is farfetched. In spite of all the circumstantial evidence, I find it hard to believe the Fed actually assassinates people."

"Perhaps some owners of the Federal Reserve eliminate anyone who tries to abolish their source of wealth." Judy shrugged. "I think it's all about money. A lot of their history suggests the owners don't want certain big sources of their money supply cut off."

"We aren't trying to abolish them or interfere with them in any way," Ben said. "But we still need to keep our eyes wide open."

Everyone was silent for a few moments.

Matt looked at Ben. "Do you think the Federal Reserve will allow you to check details in their computer system?"

"They should know we'll need to do a detailed check to do them any good," Ben said.

"What if the FBI finds some incriminating evidence in some of the files at the Federal Reserve?" Matt asked.

"It's unlikely the Federal Reserve would leave that type of information around," Ben said. "However, we'll stay on our toes. We never want to be caught off guard. We'll need to throw a lot of analytical power at the problem with the computer hacking attempts, financial and otherwise. We'll need all the analytical help we can get on every aspect of the cyber warfare stuff." He looked at Ralph. "I'd like to keep Todd and Judy involved with our analytical team."

Ralph gave a thumbs-up.

Matt narrowed his eyes. "If any of the conspiracy theories I've heard are real, you're going to need more than analytical help."

Ben gave a short laugh. "No argument there. We need to keep working together on this. Resolving the current threats is in the best interest of everyone, including Tuxtun."

"It looks like some people in the ownership hierarchy of the Federal Reserve are connected to the Illuminati and thus to the Hidden Empire," Todd said. "And I think we'll continue to be dealing with one of their action arms who handle threats to the well-being of the Hidden Empire. Right now, we think the main action arm in that regard is the Russian KGB."

"And it looks like we'll continue to deal with Hugo Wagner on all this too," Matt said.

Ben gave a slight shrug and then nodded. "Yeah, that would be an accurate statement."

"There's a lot of interaction between the World Bank and our Federal Reserve System, a lot more than I originally thought," Judy said. "Also the World Trade Organization is closely involved, as well as the International Monetary Fund. Todd and I think the main pipeline for funding the various elements of the Hidden Empire goes from the Federal Reserve through the World Bank via the IMF."

"Do you think Hugo Wagner and his partners are

directly involved in that aspect of this?" Matt asked.

Judy nodded. "Todd and I think the Hidden Empire is too. Many aspects of this boggle the mind. The more you investigate them the more complex things become. There are so many trails to follow and when you pick one and follow it you quickly come to another intersection where it splits off into thousands of more trails."

Todd nodded.

Ben's glance took in both Todd and Judy. "I've heard that statement a few times from our financial analysts at the FBI too but we all need to keep going."

"The Federal Reserve Bank of Chicago has an international finance conference every year," Judy said. "They invite researchers and policymakers from a lot of different countries."

Ben grunted. "It's clear why we need to partner with the CIA on some of this stuff."

"Yeah, the Saudis just used a wire transfer to a bank in the Channel Islands to send money to Hugo Wagner," Todd said. "Judy and I are working with some of your financial analysts and a group of CIA financial analysts on that. We're in the process of tracking all the details, including Oleg Titov's involvement and Wan FU's involvement."

"We already know the funds were earmarked for a private sector project with the International Finance Corporation of the World Bank Group." Judy scanned the faces around the table. "They were directly interacting with one of their sisters in the World Bank Group, the IBRD."

"When the World Bank Group provides money and advice to countries for economic development and eliminating poverty," Judy said, "a few insiders can throw a good smoke screen over all the advertised financing and leave no trace that some of the money actually went to an individual like Hugo Wagner."

Ben looked directly at Todd. "Do you know much about the technology these various banks are using?"

"I know a new supercomputer has been developed by China," Todd said. "And it's being used by the World Bank to move the money around."

"Do you know anything about the supercomputer?" Ben asked.

Todd nodded. "Yep, it's a Sunway Taihulight supercomputer. It's nowhere near as fast as a quantum computer but it's a lot faster than any of our conventional computers."

"We're still in the same odd position we've talked about before," Ben said. "We need to help the Federal Reserve, but we have to be leery of some owners, the descendants who might still be carrying on the work of their fathers. I hope you'll keep working on this. We need to know as much as possible about all the subtleties of the Federal Reserve and more about any groups, such as the Illuminati and the Hidden Empire, who could be actively involved. And we already know Hugo Wagner is going to be involved in a lot of the money transactions we look into."

Todd nodded his agreement.

"We've meandered a bit, but it's important to discover and stay focused on all the different aspects we're dealing with." Ben narrowed his eyes. "For now, let's get back to the main topic for this meeting."

"We might need to meander a little more to get all the known facts out on the table," Matt said. "We don't yet know how everything connects, but there's no doubt we're now dealing with an even more complex puzzle."

"And I'll bet it's even more complex than any of us think," Ben added quickly.

Matt wrinkled his brow. "Are you referring to anything specific?"

"We've been informed NSA picked up bits and pieces of a phone conversation coming from Germany into the Jacksonville area," Ben said. "Assassins were mentioned, assassins to knock off the Americans. The Hidden Empire was also mentioned."

"Any names mentioned?" Todd asked.

Ben nodded. "Roman Zak and Jonas Schulz were both mentioned, but at different times in the conversation. We think they both might be engaged in another assassination attempt."

"Do you think the targets are Ralph and me?" Matt asked.

"As far as we know you're still Hugo Wagner's main targets," Ben said. "I've requested the NRO concentrate a lot of their resources on the Jacksonville area."

"Any guesses as to what the Hidden Empire has to do with this?" Todd asked. "I don't know of any reason they would be after us."

"I was going to ask you and Judy the same question," Ben said.

Todd leaned toward Ben. "While reviewing things with one of your analytical teams, Judy and I saw some information indicating Hugo and his team had been threatened by the Hidden Empire. From all the collected intelligence Judy and I have reviewed it looks like the Hidden Empire is keeping a close eye on what

Hugo is doing."

Judy nodded. "I think the Hidden Empire doesn't want their global arrangement for monetary transactions messed up. They're probably keeping close tabs on Hugo mainly for that reason."

Matt narrowed his eyes. "We're dealing with one hell of a combination of countries, organizations, people, and issues. The United States Military needs to get involved."

"The threat matrix that's presented to the President is definitely becoming more complex," Ben said. "There are many international and domestic angles. Even if we get extra help, we must work even more closely together to try to unravel various parts of the puzzle and make progress on the resolution."

"Speaking of the threat matrix being more complicated, Cuba is directly involved in this now," Judy said. "There's a lot more collusion and there's a lot of international money involved. The drug cartels in Cuba and Mexico have hooked up with several oil cartels and they're laundering millions of dollars through shell companies and various entities in our global monetary structure."

Todd nodded. "Hugo Wagner has a connection to that and we know the Federal Reserve has connections to many of the global monetary transactions. We're trying to learn a lot more as quickly as possible but it's going to take a long time to untangle."

Ben shook his head. "Many of the Federal Reserve owners can be classified as international powers. There's no doubt a lot of shadow groups have at least some connection to them. And we know from our own experience some of those shadow groups employ what we can correctly call expert assassins."

Steve looked at Judy. "Do you know if descendants of the people who formed the Federal Reserve are still carrying on the work of their fathers?"

"I haven't yet found any direct evidence of that," Judy said, "but it's a fact that descendants of many of the original owners are still in place."

Matt noted everyone around the table had a somber expression.

"There are definitely powerful people in the shadows who don't want a big source of their money cut off," Judy said.

"And we could be messing with those people," Ben said. "We'll need to be real careful in everything we do but we can't afford to back off." He looked at Matt and Ralph. "We know Hugo Wagner wants to get you out of his way and we know Roman Zak and Jonas Schulz are in this area. You'll probably get a visit from them soon."

Ben started to say more when his cell phone vibrated. He answered.

After listening for about a minute he said a few words into his phone and then disconnected.

"NSA intercepted another phone call from Germany into this area. As usual, it was well encrypted. They haven't yet been able to decrypt a lot of it but they know Roman Zak answered the call," Ben said. "They also know Jonas Schulz is with him. NRO has multiple satellites that will be constantly in range of Jacksonville. Some have infrared capability. NRO will do a detailed scan of the area here real often and let us know if they spot Roman Zak or Jonas Schulz in the vicinity. They have the facial signatures of both of the assassins."

Matt thought about all the various aspects of what they were dealing with. Deep inside, he felt like something evil was rushing toward him and Ralph like an oncoming freight train.

"One thing for sure," Ben said, "this whole thing is as complicated as hell."

Matt gave a short laugh. "I know this isn't funny, but we can't allow ourselves to get too uptight. We have to stay reasonably loose to react properly when we have a problem."

"I agree but stay fully alert at all times," Ben said. "You and Ralph both need to guard against being overconfident. Overconfidence can get you killed. But again, I'll go along with trying to stay loose and not get too tangled up in this mess."

"No argument on that point," Matt said.

"Staying loose is going to be hard to do." Ben looked at his watch and his notes. "We have a lot more to cover in the next few hours and some of the subject matter will be even more complex."

"What threat exactly should we prepare for first?" Justin asked.

Ben looked at Matt and Ralph. "One thing I'm pretty sure about is that you're going to get a visit from some assassins very soon. Maybe all of us will. We were all attacked at the Tuxtun offices."

"Yeah, and we've made some more improvements to our security systems since Ludvig Kats tried to kill us," Ralph said.

Steve's gaze took in both Matt and Ralph. "The next attack could be at your home. Have both of you upgraded your home security systems lately?"

"We both did it right after the intrusion at Tuxtun," Ralph said. "We've added every security enhancement we think is practical."

Ben leaned toward Matt and Ralph. "We know Roman Zak and Jonas Schulz are both in the area. When you're at home keep your pistols with you at all times and stay alert."

That oncoming freight train probably will be arriving real soon, Matt thought.

Chapter 16

That evening, Matt pulled his car into his garage. His security system was programmed to recognize him and his car. If he used a different car he could remotely make appropriate changes to his system.

Matt stopped in his usual place and stayed on full alert. He closed the garage door immediately, no need to take any unnecessary chances.

As soon as he got out of the car and stood he drew his Glock 19 and kept it ready to use.

Holding his pistol, tilted upward at a forty-five-degree angle, in his right hand, he unlocked the door to his house with the key in his left hand.

Staying on full alert, Matt walked in and made a quick inspection of every room while the security system stayed on.

Due to facial recognition and other sophisticated features, the system would track him everywhere he went in the house and allow him to do things that would normally trigger an alarm.

Matt knew if he or Ralph ever got concerned about not having enough privacy they could always turn the security system off. It was their choice. Right now, with the threat of a visit from expert assassins, he figured it was best to be as secure as possible.

After he finished a thorough search of the entire house he walked to the control panel for the security system. The scanners for the yard indicated there were no detectable threats.

Matt holstered his Glock 19 and removed his phone from a pocket. He punched a button and heard Ralph answer.

"Are you home?" Matt asked.

"Yep, I just completed a search of the entire house. And the scanners for the yard show no threats. Everything appears safe at the moment. How are things with you?"

"I went through the same procedure. Things appear to be safe over here too."

"Do you think we could actually get a visit from an assassin at one or both of our homes?"

"That's likely. That's something Hugo hasn't tried yet. It's smart for us to stay prepared for that."

"Hugo might send over a sniper. Outside of our yards, we don't have the surrounding area set up with detection devices like we do at work."

"If we don't walk around outside until this threat is over we should be okay," Matt said. "We had the foresight to install bulletproof glass in all the windows in our homes and our cars when all the threats from Hugo first got started. Our parking places are secure at home and work so we shouldn't have to worry about someone planting a bomb in our cars."

"Yeah, I think we're doing all we can to stay alive. Good luck to both of us and I'll plan to see you at work tomorrow."

"Ditto," Matt said.

The call ended.

****

Later that evening, Roman Zak cautiously made his

way toward the back door of Matt Baker's home.

He stopped to check all of his hi-tech equipment. He removed a slim device the size of an iPhone from a pocket.

According to the multiple indicators, everything was working correctly. All the lights were green. No lights were yellow and none were red.

He could see his body-cam was functioning and sending images back to Hugo's fortress in Germany.

All the transmission blockers targeting Baker's security system were working. He could see no signals from him were being received by the central control unit for Baker's security system.

Roman suppressed a laugh as he resumed his movement toward the back door. This might be too easy to enjoy. He was trained to handle much bigger challenges.

He pressed a button on his control device and then reached for the doorknob and turned it.

No alarms went off.

He slowly pushed the door partially open.

Still nothing happened.

A wave of mild nausea surged through his body. This was probably going to end up being boring and he wanted to have a little fun tonight. He was addicted to things being challenging and exciting. He always met his challenges and he was proud of that.

With all the technological advantages Hugo had provided him, Matt Baker might end up being no challenge at all. He wasn't sure he liked this. It needed to be more difficult.

Roman pushed the door all the way open and walked into a utility room of sorts. A washer and a dryer were along the wall to his right. A row of shelves holding various types of containers lined the wall to his left. An open doorway was in front of him which led into a hall.

He moved into the hall and saw that it led to a large den.

Matt Baker was nowhere to be seen but Roman could hear some kitchen noises. He figured Baker was preparing something to eat.

He heard some more metallic sounds and then he heard the distinct sound of a microwave running.

Roman patted the slim control device in his pocket. He had downloaded the software last night that made him invisible to all the security monitors. It was amazing technology. As long as he kept his control device in one of his pockets, the heat detection monitors and the motion detection monitors would not detect him.

None of the other monitors would detect him either. He was invisible to everything except human sight.

Staying fully alert, Roman continued down the hallway toward the sounds. His SIG-Sauer P226 pistol was still in the holster on his right hip. He felt more comfortable that way. He could draw and fire in less than a half second. He didn't care if Baker saw him immediately. He didn't need to carry his pistol around in his hand always in a ready position.

His pistol was loaded with 9x19 Parabellum bullets. The magazine held twenty of them but one would be all he needed. He gave a slight shrug as he moved forward.

Everything was still looking too easy but he would

complete the mission and his bosses would be happy. He shrugged again, maybe he could adjust.

Roman got almost to the opening into the kitchen and stopped. He peeped around the corner of the doorway.

Baker was removing something from the microwave. His back was to Roman.

This is too easy. No fun at all.

He moved his right hand to his chest and pushed a button to switch off his body-cam. He didn't want Hugo, Oleg, or Wan yelling into his earpiece the whole time he would be trying to have a little fun. He figured they would constantly urge him to go ahead and shoot.

He reached up and switched off his earpiece too.

Now he would be able to concentrate on confronting Baker.

He waited a few seconds for Baker to put the bowl he had removed from the microwave down on the stove.

Roman noted Baker had his Glock 19 in the holster on his right hip, great. This was shaping up very nicely.

If he gave Baker a moment to recover from the surprise, this could be both productive and fun after all.

Roman certainly didn't want to miss a golden opportunity to prove to everyone what he already knew: that he was definitely the fastest gun on the planet.

Before he moved into the kitchen, Roman reached up and switched his body-cam back on. He decided he needed the video of him beating Baker in a fair fight. He knew his bosses would be yelling and screaming for him to get on with his mission, but his earpiece was turned off.

Roman decided he was going to enjoy himself as

much as he could. He wasn't going to rush.

His mission would still be accomplished. Matt Baker would still be dead and out of their way.

Chapter 17

At Ralph Gibson's house, Jonas Schulz cautiously made his way forward toward a back door close to the right side of the house.

There was also a back door leading into a screen porch.

Jonas chose the door that led directly into the house and moved toward it. As he moved, he patted the slim control device in his pocket.

He had downloaded the software last night that made him invisible to all the security monitors.

As long as he kept his control device in one of his pockets, the heat detection monitors, the motion detection monitors, and none of the other monitors could detect he was there.

When he got to the back door, he stopped to check all of his hi-tech equipment.

According to the multiple indicators, everything was working correctly. All the lights were green.

He could see his body-cam was functioning and sending images and sound back to Hugo's fortress.

All the transmission blockers targeting Gibson's security system were working. He could tell no signals from him were being received by the central control unit for Gibson's security system.

Jonas smiled. Things were looking good.

He pressed a button on his control device and then

reached for the doorknob on the back door.

He turned it.

No alarms went off, good.

After he opened the door a little wider, Jonas took a deep breath and exhaled slowly as he walked inside.

Everything looked okay and he continued forward into a small storage room with an open door ahead revealing a hallway.

He knew the slim control device in his pocket was giving out signals to keep him invisible to all the security monitors.

The capability Hugo and his group had provided to him was unbelievable and he was enjoying it fully.

Staying alert, Jonas moved forward to the hallway and peeped around the corner to his left.

No one was in the hallway and all was quiet.

He quickly looked to his right.

All was clear that way too.

Jonas scanned the hallway again in both directions. No one was in the immediate area.

He moved his right arm straight up and tightened his finger on the trigger of the silenced Heckler & Koch USP he carried in his right hand.

As soon as he spotted Gibson, he would kill him and complete his assignment quickly. The magazine in his pistol held 15 bullets.

They were all 9x19 mm Parabellum cartridges. He should only need one of them but it was always good to have more if something unexpected happened.

He scanned the hallway again. Everything was still clear. He turned to his left toward the center of the house and moved down the hallway.

In a few more seconds he heard some sounds. It

quickly became obvious the TV was on.

With all of his hi-tech security, Gibson certainly isn't expecting any surprises. He's probably relaxing on his couch and looking forward to some more entertainment and a good night's rest.

Jonas felt almost gleeful. This was all working perfectly, as planned.

Jonas kept his silenced Heckler & Koch USP in his right hand and pointed forward. He kept his finger tight on the trigger as he continued toward the sound of the TV.

He planned to stay on full alert until this assignment was over and he had left the premises.

Jonas moved slowly forward. He would be ready to fire as soon as he saw Gibson.

****

After Matt had placed the bowl he had removed from the microwave on the stove, he turned to get a spoon.

However, what awaited him was a massive surprise.

Standing about five feet away from him, a muscular figure grinned widely.

The man's right hip held a holstered pistol, and his hand poised inches away, in a ready position.

Matt recognized him as Roman Zak from photos he had seen.

It was definitely a sudden shock but Matt had experienced plenty of sudden shocks before. He had always recovered quickly.

Roman jiggled the fingers on his right hand. "I would advise you not to go for your pistol right now. You'll probably have a better chance later. I always want to be fair." He continued to grin.

"What do you want?" Matt asked.

"Maybe just to have a little fun before you die," Roman said. "This is too easy and a little boring." His grin stayed intact as he continued to jiggle his fingers.

Matt narrowed his eyes and didn't comment, glad he hadn't been shot in the back.

"You have quite a reputation with my bosses for being a top gun but I know I'm better and I'm here to prove it," Roman said. "I'm going to give you a chance to fully recover from your shock and then participate in a fast-draw contest. I want you to be at your best." Roman's grin widened.

"How did you get in here?" Matt asked. "I have the best security system available."

"It's obviously not good enough," Roman said. "Hugo Wagner's technology far exceeds yours." He laughed for several seconds. "That's one reason I like working for him."

Matt studied the assassin for a moment. It was obvious Roman wanted to taunt him for a little while. All these Russian guys seemed to have a big ego. Matt felt a strong surge of relief.

Roman looked directly at Matt and continued to grin. It was obvious Roman was getting a lot of pleasure out of the situation.

Roman maintained a perfectly balanced stance as he continued to jiggle the fingers on his right hand. He looked at Matt and said, "Hugo feels you were primarily responsible for wreaking his operations in Jacksonville. He's looking forward to you being out of his way."

Matt remained quiet, assessing his options.

"You're not nearly as good or as smart as you think you are, Baker. I just want to make sure you know that before you die."

Matt waited to see what Roman was going to do. He had gradually improved his position to execute his fast draw if Roman reached for his weapon. He wasn't jiggling his fingers like Roman was doing but he was as ready as he could be.

"Okay, Baker, here we are," Roman said with a grin. "It's time to meet your maker. I've never lost a gunfight and I'm not going to lose this one. I'll let you get in the best position you can and then we'll draw. Let me know when you're ready."

Matt figured Roman was wearing bulletproof clothing so he would aim for his head. That would take another fraction of a second to pull the trigger.

Roman continued to jiggle the fingers on his right hand as he looked directly at his target.

Matt didn't move. He stayed perfectly still for several more seconds while Roman glared at him.

"Okay, any damn time you're ready," Roman blurted out with a hint of irritation.

Matt still didn't move but he stayed ready to draw if Roman made any motion toward his pistol.

"You're not going to chicken out on me, are you?" Roman asked impatiently. "I need to beat you in a fair fight."

Matt drew and fired.

Roman's head bent backward from the impact of the 9mm bullet as he dropped straight to the floor.

Matt instantly knew his plan had worked perfectly. Roman was definitely dead.

He had waited until just the right moment to draw.

He knew Roman was becoming more irritated every second he had to wait.

Matt immediately grabbed his phone and hit a button.

He needed to check on Ralph.

The phone kept ringing.

Come on, pick up.

He immediately disconnected and punched the emergency button for Justin. A police detail needed to pick up Roman Zak's body and another detail needed to rush to Ralph's house and check on things.

After talking to Justin, Matt called Ben.

Chapter 18

Ralph moved suddenly in his easy chair and reached for his ringing phone.

At that instant, a bullet tore into the wall at the exact spot where his head had been.

"Don't answer that phone," a voice filled with menace warned.

Ralph looked behind him.

A man stood in the opening from the hallway with a pistol pointed in Ralph's direction.

He immediately recognized the man as Jonas Schulz from photos he had seen.

"What do you want?" Ralph asked.

The man laughed. "That should be obvious." He shifted the end of the barrel of his pistol toward Ralph.

Ralph dove for the floor as another bullet whizzed by him. He rolled toward the back of the couch and got behind it.

Ralph crawled to the far end of the couch and drew his Glock 19 from the holster on his right hip.

As Ralph peeped around the corner of the couch, another bullet whizzed by and slammed into a cabinet, just inches from his head.

Ralph drew back immediately, but he had registered Schultz's position.

If he had held on to his phone, he could have been calling for help.

Now what was he going to do?

Ralph stayed flat on the floor and listened carefully. The only sound he could hear was the TV. He figured Jonas would be moving to a new position, but in which direction? He decided to take another peek in a few more seconds and try to spot him.

Staying in a crawling position, Ralph turned toward the other end of the couch. Maybe it would catch Jonas by surprise if he popped up over there. Maybe he could get off a shot at Jonas before he got shot at again.

As Ralph crawled toward the new position, he tightly gripped his Glock 19, ready to shoot. He kept glancing behind him as he moved, no telling where Jonas would show up next.

Ralph got to the other end of the couch and got in position to shoot fast. He would pop his head out from the corner of the couch quickly and try to spot Jonas.

Ralph held his pistol in a ready position and popped his head out a few inches from the corner of the couch.

Jonas was nowhere to be seen.

Ralph pulled his head back immediately and looked behind him down the length of the couch.

No one was there.

He stayed on high alert. He needed to make a decision.

Should he hold his position or try to get to another room?

While he was thinking, the sound of sirens in the distance reached his ears.

The sounds got louder quickly.

In another few seconds, they stopped.

Banging sounds came from the front door and all the alarms went off in the house.

Ralph felt a wave of relief flow through him. Whoever had called earlier had apparently sounded the alarm. Not only had help arrived but Jonas had to be distracted.

It was time to take another chance.

Keeping his pistol in firing position, Ralph popped his head up above the back of the couch.

He immediately saw Jonas a few yards from his previous position, turned toward the front door, looking in that direction.

Ralph fired multiple shots quickly. He didn't like shooting someone in the back, but this was the only choice he had.

Jonas stumbled sideways but remained on his feet. He turned back toward Ralph, his pistol into position to return fire.

He's wearing bulletproof clothing. He quickly fired rounds at the assassin's head.

With a loud thud, Jonas dropped hard to the floor.

A swarm of people rushed onto the scene. All the ones in front were in uniform, with rifles rotating left and right.

"It's okay!" Ralph yelled. "I got him and I think he was the only one."

The alarms continued blaring.

"We'll search the house anyway," the leader of the group yelled. He waved to his team members.

The group separated and spread in all directions, their rifles in position to fire if necessary as they began the search.

Ralph switched off the alarm system.

Matt, Justin, and Ben all converged on Ralph.

A wave of relief coursed through Ralph, glad to still be alive.

Chapter 19

Matt walked up to Ralph and gave him a light punch on the shoulder.

"You had me worried," Matt said.

"I figured it was you who called. Glad you took immediate action." Ralph gestured toward Justin and Ben.

Matt nodded as a clean-up crew carrying a variety of equipment and two uniformed policemen rushed in.

One policeman carried a body bag.

In a few moments, Vince opened the front door and entered the house with his pistol in his hand, ready to fire. After taking a few steps into the house he put his pistol back in the holster and rushed toward Matt and the group around him.

As Vince came up to the group, Justin said, "Welcome to the discussion. We just beat you here and just starting to sort through what happened."

"Glad things are under control," Vince blurted out.

Ralph looked at Matt. "You can see what happened here. What happened at your house?"

"A little different," Matt said. "I was in the kitchen removing my dinner from the microwave when suddenly Roman Zak was behind me."

Justin grunted. "I guess with all the added security enhancements you guys had installed neither one of you thought you would have any undetected company."

"That's exactly correct in my case," Matt said.

Ralph pressed his lips together and nodded vigorously. "Same here, total surprise."

"I was really lucky Roman had a big ego just like Ludvig," Matt said. "He could have finished me off easily but he wanted to prove he could draw faster than I could. He obviously felt he was the fastest gun on the planet and wanted another chance to demonstrate that." Matt shrugged. "I don't have that problem. I don't care whether I'm the fastest or not, so I cheated a little bit."

Everyone looked curiously at Matt.

"Roman gave me the rules for how things were supposed to proceed for us to have a fair contest," Matt said. "He gave me a chance to make sure I was in position and then he wanted me to tell him when I was ready."

Ben narrowed his eyes. "So you didn't tell him you were ready. You just drew and fired."

"Yeah," Matt said. "I guess for some reason he thought I would honor the rules he put down for what he considered would be a fair fight." He shrugged. "He had a body cam on his chest and I'm sure he wanted to use the video to prove he had given me a fair chance to draw. He obviously wanted to be able to advertise his victory and enhance his claim to be the fastest gun on the planet." Matt gave a short laugh. "And again, I don't have that problem. I couldn't care less about having the reputation of being the fastest gun."

After the SWAT team gave the all-clear and left with the cleanup team along with two policemen who carried away the body bag, Ralph gave the details of his experience.

Matt added some more details about his encounter

with Roman.

After a brief silence, Ben said, "Well we now know more about the capability Hugo Wagner has. And we still have to cope with it." He looked at Matt and Ralph. "It's good you both were following the recommendation to constantly wear your pistols around your house." He focused his gaze directly on Ralph. "In your case in particular it probably saved your life."

Ralph and everyone else nodded.

"Well, after this, it's going to be hard to get back to business as usual but we need to do that," Ben said. "And we need to remember the danger isn't necessarily over for tonight."

Justin nodded. "I plan to leave guards outside both houses for the next few nights. Maybe we'll figure out some new ways to enhance the security systems during that time."

Vince looked at Justin. "I'll help you with the guard service. I'll shift one of my nighttime patrols over to one of the houses."

Justin nodded. "Okay, put them at Ralph's house. I'll cover Matt's."

"Good," Ben said. "We all need a good night's sleep. I've already mentioned we need to get back to business as usual and something has come up that we need to do tomorrow morning." He looked at Vince and Justin. "I'll post a guard at our houses too. We know Hugo is a vindictive maniac. He might also come after us for revenge on what happened tonight."

Everyone nodded as they looked at Ben and waited for him to provide the details.

"We know Hugo Wagner has an international team of expert engineers who help him perfect the capability he has with his computers, satellites, and such," Ben said. "I've been trying to get more help in combating all that capability and I just got an urgent message a few minutes ago relative to some of the help I've requested."

Matt kept his gaze fixed on Ben while he waited for the forthcoming information.

"We know Wagner makes good use of his quantum computer and I'm sure he used it to unravel every detail of the security systems we've installed at our homes, office buildings, and parking areas." Ben glanced around at everyone. "A few days ago, I found out the Department of Homeland Security has a special project going on at the University of Florida to study and experiment with quantum computing."

Everybody remained silent, waiting for Ben to continue.

"I've been informed we can get a tour of the project tomorrow morning if we want it," Ben said. "I think it will be an opportunity for us to understand more thoroughly the unbelievable capability Hugo has access to and so I accepted the invitation. They've developed two quantum computers and they're going to give us a demonstration of what they can do."

"What kind of demonstration?" Matt asked.

"I asked that question," Ben said. "I was told they would explain everything tomorrow and that the demonstration should be conducive to more thoroughly understanding the capability of quantum computing."

Justin nodded. "That should be useful information when we're doing more of our planning."

Ben looked at Ralph and Matt. "You guys have just been through a nerve-shattering experience. I would advise you not to go if you don't think you're up to it."

Matt gave a short laugh and looked at Ralph.

"Ever since we've been working alongside law enforcement, we've been through a lot of similar experiences," Ralph said. "I think you can consider us hardened veterans now. There's no way we want to miss the demo tomorrow."

"Just checking," Ben said with a grin.

"And while we're on the subject, did they give you any limit to the number of people you could bring?" Ralph asked.

"They never mentioned any limit but I'm sure they wouldn't want a crowd to show up," Ben said.

"Think we could add three more?" Ralph asked.

Ben raised an eyebrow. "Who do you have in mind?"

"Judy, Todd, and Steve," Ralph said. "I think it would be good for our financial expert, our technical expert, and our security chief at Tuxtun to see the demo firsthand and not just hear about it from us. They would probably be a big help to us when we're discussing any additional knowledge we pick up."

Justin looked directly at Ben. "I think that's an excellent idea."

"Anyone have any additional comments?" Ben asked.

No one said anything.

"I guess eight of us wouldn't be too big of a crowd," Ben said. "I'll let them know how many of us are coming and see if I get any pushback."

"Do you have someone you can call now and ask?" Matt asked. "It would be good to give Judy, Todd, and Steve a heads-up."

Ben nodded as he removed his phone from a pocket and punched in a number. After a short conversation, he reported that eight people would be an acceptable number.

After notifying Judy, Todd, and Steve and completing a short wrap-up conversation, everyone prepared to get some rest.

Chapter 20

In their hi-tech fortress in southern Germany, Hugo, Oleg, and Wan sat in three of the four chairs in the center portion of the control room.

Jake Bolton sat in the fourth chair.

"What a damn turn of events," Hugo said.

A brief silence ensued.

Hugo slammed his right fist on the desk and turned to look at Oleg. "Do all your Russian assassins have such damned big egos they can't do their jobs?"

Before Oleg could answer Hugo continued, "Roman and Ludvig each had a golden opportunity to complete their mission but their egos got in their way." He slammed his fist on the desk again.

"Jonas didn't complete his mission either," Oleg said.

Hugo narrowed his eyes. "But it wasn't due to his ego. He just had some bad luck that stemmed from Roman not doing his job. Had Baker not been alive to make that phone call, Jonas would have eliminated Gibson."

Oleg remained silent.

"Well, we can't change the past, but we still have a lot of capability to get rid of our enemies," Hugo said. He took a deep breath and exhaled slowly. "We'll continue forward and try to make some progress on the things we need to get done." Hugo looked at Jake. "You mentioned you got another message from the Hidden Empire."

Jake nodded. "And it was the same one. They don't want you screwing up the world's gold supply and they don't want you firing any missiles into the United States. They asked me to clearly communicate that to you and to tell you this was your last warning."

"There's no way they could know I'm still planning to do that," Hugo said. He gave Jake a long stare.

Jake shrugged. "They told me they're keeping up with everything you're doing and if you continue to ignore the rules they've laid down they'll wipe you off the planet."

Hugo laughed. "They had better worry about my eliminating *them*." He made a sweeping motion with his right hand toward all the images and data on the multiple displays around the room. "You can see how much data we have on display right at this moment. We can instantly have millions of pieces of information as soon as we get a few more specifics about them. There's no way they can hide from us."

Jake gave another shrug and didn't comment.

"But they still seem to be okay with my activity to eliminate Baker and Gibson?" Hugo asked.

"They haven't mentioned that as being a problem," Jake said. "And we all know they have to be very aware of the ongoing activity in that regard."

"Exactly how was that last message you got from them delivered?" Hugo asked.

"Everything was the same as the times before except a different man showed up," Jake said. "It seems they never send the same person twice."

Hugo narrowed his eyes and leaned toward Jake. "Any clue this time about where the man came from or what nationality he was?"

"I pay close attention to everything and there was absolutely nothing different other than the individual." He spoke English like the other guys, and none of them had any accent."

Hugo grunted. "And, like I've mentioned before, none of the people I've spoken to on the phone had an accent either."

Jake hesitated a moment and then said, "In the five-minute conversation we had, he emphasized three different times that you're absolutely forbidden to go after the gold or to shoot a missile into the United States. He told me to make sure it was clear to you that neither of those things will be tolerated."

Hugo laughed again. "Let them try. If they can find us they'll discover all my defenses are stronger than they think they are."

Oleg stared at Hugo. "So you're going to continue to go after the gold and you'll destroy places in the United States with missiles when you choose to do so, right?"

"Yeah, I think their space program needs to be eliminated and I'm going to destroy all the sites where they're working on it," Hugo said. "Several tactical nuclear missiles should do the job."

Wan and Jake also stared at Hugo.

"No one is as powerful as we are. We don't have to back down from anybody. We'll do what we want to," Hugo said.

"But again, maybe the Hidden Empire has powerful technology we don't know about," Wan cautioned.

"You keep reminding me of that but I keep telling you that's not possible." Hugo narrowed his eyes. "It's obvious to me they're bluffing. There's no way they can destroy us even if they, by some chance, find out where we are. Our security cannot be penetrated, even if they shoot missiles at us. We have an anti-missile defense that can block any attack."

"I still think it's strange that English has been the only language the Hidden Empire has used so far. We need to keep that in mind." Jake glanced at Hugo. "The fact that our group is from Germany, Russia, and China respectively should have prompted them to use some other language. I'm still surprised they didn't speak to you in German when you were talking to them on the phone."

Hugo shrugged.

Wan looked at Jake. "Did the last man who paid you a visit mention anything about Hugo needing to call them again?"

"That subject didn't come up. He just kept emphasizing I needed to warn Hugo about going after the gold and about making plans to hit the United States with a missile."

Wan nodded slowly and glanced at Oleg.

"I don't have anything to add," Oleg said. "I think we've covered everything well enough."

Hugo leaned toward Jake. "Do you have anything else to say?"

"I've delivered the message and answered a lot of questions," Jake said. "I agree with Oleg. I think we've covered everything."

"Okay, you did your job. We'll go through our

normal exit procedure." Hugo pressed a button on his phone.

Someone quickly arrived to escort Jake out of the control room in the manner they used to keep the location of the facility secret from their enemies.

Hugo glanced at Oleg and Wan. "Well, we need to decide what we want to concentrate on the most. We have several priorities now. We still need to eliminate Baker and Gibson, we want to get the gold, we want to eliminate more obstacles to our world conquest, and we want to put more work into finding additional information about the Hidden Empire. My choice is to still concentrate on eliminating Baker and Gibson first. I'm not going to be able to rest until I get them out of my way."

"I have a couple of good assassins available right now," Wan said. "They're fully capable of killing people with their bare hands. I think we ought to use them next."

Hugo looked at Wan. "Yeah, you mentioned them before. Tell me about them again."

Wan described the assassins' merits and experience.

"I also have another option available right now," Hugo said. "I still have one of my expert German assassins in place and ready to go. His name is Lucas Becker. Among his many skills, he's an excellent sniper. We might give that a try. We'll discuss this in more detail for a few minutes and develop a plan. Then we'll put our plan in motion right away."

The discussion lasted for almost an hour.

"Well, I think we've analyzed this in just about every possible way and we'll first give Wan a chance to use his assassins to eliminate Baker and Gibson," Hugo said. "If it doesn't work, we'll try using a sniper next. Surely we can succeed in eliminating Baker and Gibson soon."

Oleg and Wan nodded.

Wan looked at Hugo. "I think you're going to be pleased with how well my assassins perform. Ho Cham and Chung Lin have never failed on an assignment." He grabbed his secure satellite phone. "It'll take a couple of days for them to get in position. I'll give them their instructions." He punched a number into his phone.

****

In an elaborate castle located about twenty miles east of Zurich, Switzerland an important conversation was in progress. Three elder men sat in cushioned chairs in the plush lounge area where they usually gathered to discuss important business matters that needed immediate attention.

As members of the Illuminati, they were important factors in helping to make decisions relative to maintaining control over a lot of world events.

"Zeus, Jupiter, and Odin have some big decisions to make and they want our opinion," Vulcan said as he filled his pipe with his favorite almond-blend tobacco.

"Are you communicating with them directly?" Apollo asked.

Vulcan lit his pipe and took a puff as he narrowed his eyes and looked at Apollo.

"No," Vulcan said. "I'm communicating directly with Thor like I usually do. We always maintain the utmost secrecy no matter what circumstances we're involved in." He took a long puff from his pipe. "Thor assured me all the information we need to make a decision is available."

After filling his pipe with his favorite cherry-blend tobacco, Neptune flicked his lighter and positioned the flame. He quickly took a puff and nodded slowly. "Yes, I think we have a clear picture of what's going on with Hugo Wagner and his organization."

Apollo didn't comment.

"It's clear Hugo Wagner hasn't changed his plans," Vulcan said. "It's obvious he's still going to interfere with the global money flow. He's now been warned twice. My opinion is that he needs to be eliminated and his entire operation destroyed before he does any big damage."

"Do you think we should make him more aware of our capability and give him one more warning?" Apollo asked.

"I don't think that's a good idea," Vulcan said. "If he does change his mind, he'll know more about us than we want anyone outside of our organization to know."

Neptune nodded slowly. "I agree with that."

Apollo didn't argue.

"Big changes in the global monetary system would affect us in a very negative way," Vulcan said. "We couldn't continue to operate the way we do now. So it's clear we can't let Hugo Wagner go ahead with his plans. We have to eliminate him."

"We know Hugo has a very secure setup. Other than us, he has the best technology on the planet." Neptune took a long puff from his pipe and leaned forward. "I still worry there's a chance we might not be able to stop him."

"Remember we know exactly where he is and we

have a lot of options," Vulcan said. "The Russian KGB has access to a lot of nuclear weapons, all types. We can use a tactical nuke which won't leave a lot of radioactive fallout. We can destroy him and his whole setup very easily. We can completely wipe him off the face of the earth if we choose to." He took a long slow puff from his pipe. "And I vote we go ahead and do that."

After a slight hesitation, Neptune and Apollo each gave a thumbs-up.

"I'll go ahead and tell Thor what we decided but I won't tell him we think it must be done immediately," Vulcan said. "I'm sure our leaders will choose the right timing."

Chapter 21

The next morning, Ben, Justin, Vince, Matt, Ralph, Judy, Todd, and Steve arrived at a remote location on one edge of the campus at the University of Florida in Gainesville.

They arrived in two SUVs. The five people from Tuxtun came together while the three lawmen came in an FBI vehicle.

After the vehicles were parked in a lot about fifty feet from the two-story stucco building painted gray, everyone got out and walked toward the two glass doors at the front entrance.

Matt figured the glass on the doors was probably bulletproof.

Two men wearing long white coats met the group at the front door and introduced themselves only as Carl and George.

Matt assumed they had a good reason for that. Even though everyone in his group had a top-secret clearance, he figured the two men wanted to keep everything as secret as possible, including their identities, which, based on the nature of their work, made a lot of sense.

Carl and George ushered them into a large room with a variety of large mainframe computers. Some were odd looking.

"We've developed two quantum computers and

they're now both fully functional," Carl said. "Each is a billion times faster than the best supercomputer. We gave our bosses a demo yesterday."

"We all have top-secret clearances," Ben said. "Could you tell us who your bosses are?"

George shrugged. "We've verified your clearances, but we've been advised we can't do that. That's on a need-to-know basis only. We've been authorized to give you this demonstration because our bosses feel the knowledge you gain will be beneficial in helping you cope with some of the challenges you're facing. They feel a better knowledge of quantum computing as well as a general knowledge of what we're doing here will be useful to you."

Ben gave a short laugh. "They're right about that being useful to us." He looked at Carl and George. "Thank you for doing this."

Both men nodded.

"Our bosses have been concerned about all aspects of our national banking system, especially the Federal Reserve part, for almost ten years now," George said. "And they procured a large federal grant to develop more protection for the money flow in our banking systems."

Carl nodded. "George and I both started with this program ten years ago and we've made a lot of progress." He waved everyone toward a large steel door. "Follow us. We have some interesting things to show you."

Everyone followed the two men wearing the white lab coats.

Carl opened the large steel door and led everyone into another large room which was occupied by two huge odd-looking black machines.

"These quantum computers are designed with a completely different set of guidelines than normal computers use," Carl said. "Our crew here built them with help from several universities and private corporations."

"How do they work?" Todd asked.

"They operate on the Superposition Principle," Carl said. "That relates to atoms being in several different energy states at once. Each computer can act on all variable states simultaneously, carrying out numerous computations in parallel."

George nodded. "A lot of complicated calculations will be done instantly. Each computer is a billion times faster than the best supercomputer. The speed you'll be exposed to in a few minutes will be hard to comprehend."

"How much speed is that?" Matt asked.

"Do you know what a petaflop is?" George gave all of the people in Ben's group a curious stare.

"A thousand trillion floating point operations per second," Todd said. "We've all been versed on many aspects of quantum computing."

"You're right." George smiled. "And the fastest supercomputer in the world can run at a little over two petaflops."

"The quantum computers we've developed are a billion times faster than that," Carl said. "We're using molecules that interact with one another as qubits. Each molecule consists of the nuclei from five fluorine and two carbon atoms. The atoms operate on the Superposition Principle I just mentioned."

"So what are you going to show us?" Todd asked.

His glance took in both computer scientists.

Matt noted the hint of impatience from Todd didn't seem to bother either of the scientists.

"Thanks to a lot of help from various experts in applying some finishing touches over the last few weeks, we've worked out a method to protect our Federal Reserve System." George hesitated. "But I don't think you want me to go over all the mathematical and financial details."

"Just give us the bottom line," Ben said. "None of us, other than Todd, know a lot about quantum computing."

George shrugged. "We can now protect the Federal Reserve System."

Ben gave a short laugh. "We might need a little more information than that."

George flashed a ghost of a smile. "We're using some very sophisticated math combined with our financial operations. We even use something called quantum regression. Bottom line, we can block anyone's attempt to break into our financial systems, even if they're using a quantum computer themselves."

A brief silence ensued. Everyone in Ben's group was obviously waiting for the two scientists to continue.

"We've prepared a demo," Carl said. He signaled to George.

George flipped a switch. Several lights blinked on the two sets of hardware. A low hum ensued from the quantum computers. After two large monitors came to life, each displaying 'ready,' Carl tapped a few keys and took a step back.

A laser printer spat out a sheet of paper. Carl

grabbed the report and waved everyone to a large table. After placing the page on the top of the table, he pointed to a large digital number with a dollar sign.

"That's our measurement of our actual national money supply," Carl said. "Most experts disagree with each other. They all seem to have different ways of defining money." He looked toward Judy. "Would you agree that this multi-trillion dollar figure is about right?"

Judy grunted. "If we're only talking about the actual amount, it should be in the ballpark."

"We have a large database that includes all the data the Federal Reserve publishes plus other data we've developed from our extensive research," Carl said. "M3 is the broadest measure of money supply, but the Federal Reserve stopped publishing M3 in March 2006. They said it didn't convey any further useful information than M2. However, George and I did our own data collection. We've compiled an accurate database representing M3."

"How did you do that?" Judy asked.

"The technical and financial details are immense," Carl said. "I'll just say we have a lot of financial experts and scientists working together who furnish a lot of support for our project here."

George nodded. "This discussion should never be mentioned to anyone else unless we authorize it."

"We'll all be careful," Ben said.

George stepped forward and punched on one of the keyboards. 'Run M-Plus Power Play' appeared on the monitor of one computer. George hit the Enter key for that program.

Everyone in Ben's group watched with interest.

The words 'Program Blocked' instantly appeared on the other monitor.

Pointing toward the message, George said, "This quantum computer was playing defense."

"You were running a program similar to what you think hackers would run?" Todd raised an eyebrow and stared at George.

"You got it," George said.

"What type of simulation are you using?" Todd asked.

George gestured toward Carl. "You tell them."

"Hard to explain in normal terms," Carl said. "Let's just say on the first computer we're simulating the best way we can devise for someone to hack into the Federal Reserve System. On the second computer, we're trying to block what the first computer does."

"Who designed the programs?" Judy asked.

"Our team of experts, which includes George and me," Carl said. "Our defensive program covers trillions of possibilities. We think we can block any program a hacker would use, even if they have a quantum computer."

George nodded. "Carl and I, along with the other members of the team, have worked hard on this for a long time."

"What about other members of your team leaking something?" Matt asked.

"They're all acutely aware of the sensitive nature of this stuff," Carl said. "We've worked together for years. We've never had a problem."

"Is your program ready to use on the real system?" George asked.

Carl grunted. "I think so. We just ran it on the

actual Federal Reserve System."

Matt saw a lot of eyes widen. He was sure his did.

"You broke into our Federal Reserve System?" Judy asked.

"Good thing we're honest people," Carl said. He grinned.

George nodded. He also grinned.

Judy shook her head. "So your defensive system is already installed?" She stared at the two scientists.

"In a manner of speaking, yes," Carl said.

"Do any authorities know about this?" Matt asked.

"Only our bosses and a few other people and now your group," Carl said. "You all have top-secret clearances. We decided to let you know."

"Is it okay to let my boss know?" Ben asked.

"We're counting on it," Carl said. "That was a big reason we wanted you to get a firsthand demonstration."

Ben's gaze took in both Carl and George. "Thanks for the session. We'll make sure all the right people know about the protection being in place."

Carl and George each gave a thumbs-up. "We want the heads of the FBI and CIA to put in some good words for us up the line. Our enemies will make improvements to their technology and we'll need to do the same. We need to keep our funding." They waved everyone toward the front entrance.

Matt now understood Carl's and George's motivation for spending time with them.

On the way out, Ben said to his group, "Going forward, we must execute properly on multiple fronts. To do that, we have to be fully prepared for a wide range of contingencies."

Matt gave a sarcastic laugh. "Yeah, should be no problem. We're only dealing with a small number of issues."

Everyone else laughed too.

Matt knew everyone wanted to stay loose. You could operate a lot better if you weren't all tensed up.

****

In his hi-tech fortress in southern Germany, Hugo Wagner sat in one of the four chairs in the center portion of the control room.

Oleg and Wan sat in two of the other chairs.

They all were concentrating on an image of a broad area outside a building on the University of Florida campus, the building Matt and his group had gone into.

Hugo narrowed his eyes and leaned toward Wan. "Are your assassins wearing body-cams?"

"I didn't think a body-cam was necessary in this case but I did go ahead and send them the bulletproof clothing," Wan said. "I even sent them the bulletproof helmets you suggested."

Hugo nodded. "Good decision. It's good to be absolutely sure a hail of bullets won't take them out."

Wan gestured toward the displays on the walls and focused the red dot from his laser pointer on one of them. "You can see we have all the detail we need from the satellite images. Since everything will occur outside, we'll have all the video we need."

"My Russian engineers developed this part of our technology," Oleg said. "We can each have our own display in tremendous detail. We can zoom in and out to get whatever look we want and we can record everything for analysis later." He flashed a big grin. "We'll have everything we want to know. We can keep up with everything that goes on."

"Can we talk to them?" Hugo asked.

Wan nodded. "Each assassin has a small hi-tech microphone and an earpiece. We can communicate directly with them if we need to." He held his right hand up. "However, I don't think we should call them much. It would be too distracting."

Hugo grunted but made no comment.

Wan hesitated a moment and then said, "But remember, we can call them if we get into a situation where it's obvious talking with them would be useful."

Hugo narrowed his eyes and stared at Wan. "So you have no argument with our communicating with them if it looks to be necessary?"

"I'm okay with it when we think it's necessary, but remember I don't want to distract them," Wan said. "I have this mission set up to succeed."

Hugo nodded slowly.

Wan looked at Hugo. "Ho and Chung are experts on this type of ambush. They have a couple of AK-56 rifles if they choose to use them. They'll form a good plan and they'll make adjustments if they need to change anything when the action starts. They're probably discussing details and fine-tuning their plan right now."

Wan focused a red dot on the area the Chinese assassins were in. "If you look closely, you can see one of them behind some bushes."

"I see him and he's not wearing a helmet," Hugo said.

"They're probably waiting until the action is ready to start," Wan said. "They can put them on within a couple of seconds."

"It's risky to wait." Hugo stared at Wan. "You can never predict how quickly things might evolve."

"I'm allowing them to make their own decisions," Wan said.

Hugo shrugged. "Okay, your choice, now how do I set up my own private display that only I can control?"

Wan looked at the displays on the wall and spoke some instructions to the artificial intelligence in control of the super-sophisticated software system.

In a few more seconds, the three of them each had their own private display that only he could control with the device he had in his hand.

Wan gave Oleg and Hugo a quick lesson in using their control devices.

Hugo focused his laser pointer on his own private display and began manipulating the images.

Oleg and Wan did the same.

After a few minutes of testing, Hugo said. "Okay, I got it. This is great." He looked at Wan. "I'll not interfere with their thinking or their activity. I'll leave it up to you to contact them if you think there's any need to do so."

Wan nodded and raised his right fist straight up into the air in a victory salute.

Oleg did the same.

"I'll wait and see how they do," Hugo said. He narrowed his eyes and pressed his lips together.

****

Ho Cham and Chung Li huddled in a secluded area on the University of Florida campus close to where their targets' SUVs were parked.

They both assumed a crouched position behind a row of bushes. Each man was almost seven feet tall,

176

and if they stood, their heads would tower above the bushes, making them very obvious to anyone looking in their direction.

Chung thought that when their targets returned to their vehicles, they would undoubtedly be scanning the area, including their direction.

Chung looked at the two AK-56 rifles lying on the ground beside them. The AK-56 was a Chinese-produced version of the AK-47. It used the same ammunition, but it had some improvements both the Chinese assassins liked.

"Think we should use the rifles and just make this a regular ambush?" Chung asked.

"We'll keep that in mind as this situation progresses. We can make a quick decision at any time," Ho said. He stayed in his crouched position and peered through a hole in the bush he was behind at the two-story gray building.

"According to Wan, there are eight of them," Ho said. "If we start shooting early and don't get all of them instantly, some of them are going to shoot back quickly and we know they all are expert marksmen."

"Yeah, good point."

Ho shrugged. "So what do you think?"

Chung studied the area between them and the building.

"Bushes line both sides of the walkway leading to the vehicles they're going to get into," Chung said. "If we start firing and they drop straight down, they'll be hidden from our sight."

Ho nodded but didn't comment.

"I don't know if we can kill all eight of them quickly enough to avoid receiving return fire," Chung said. "And we certainly don't have any real cover, nothing that will stop bullets from hitting us. We're wearing the bullet-proof clothing Wan sent us but our heads aren't protected."

A brief silence ensued.

"I feel more comfortable letting them get real close to their vehicles and then pouncing out from the bushes and killing them with our bare hands," Chung said. "We're certainly trained to do that and we've had a lot of experience using our main expertise."

"Remember, there are eight of them and we know Baker is an exceptionally fast draw."

"One of us should go after Baker first thing."

"That would be you," Ho said. "You're the best. I'll go after Gibson. I think he's almost as good as Baker. We need to get both of them out of the way instantly and then we'll deal with the others."

"There will still be six left to deal with, and we know at least the three lawmen are experts with their pistols."

"Even if the bullet-proof suits don't work as advertised, we know we can handle being shot a few times without the bullets penetrating our multiple layers of thick muscle and slowing us down."

Chung nodded. "I think we have a plan. We'll let them get close to their vehicles and I'll jump out from behind the bushes first and go after Baker. You follow behind me and go after Gibson."

"I'll let you get their attention, and then I'll rush out when they aren't expecting me."

Chung wrinkled his brow. "What does that mean?"

He gave a dismissive wave. "Let's not waste time discussing details about that. I want to catch them by surprise that there's two of us, that's all." He pointed toward the building. "Let's get ready to execute. Wan just notified us they're coming out."

Chung tilted his head slightly and nodded.

Chapter 22

Matt walked out of the front entrance of the building and stayed on high alert. Ralph followed behind him.

They had planned their exit procedure and were prepared for an ambush. Matt and Ralph went first because they were the best warriors in the group and would probably have the quickest reaction to trouble.

Matt went to the right of the walkway.

Ralph moved to the left while the other six people delayed a moment and headed down the center of the walkway toward the parking lot.

Matt and Ralph stayed in front of the group as they all hurried toward the two vehicles.

Everyone scanned the area as their training had taught them.

So far everything looked okay, Matt thought. But he stayed on full alert as they moved forward. He noted everyone was staying on full alert and continuously scanning the surrounding area.

As the group stepped over the curb and onto the edge of the parking lot, Matt saw a huge man emerge from behind a bush a few yards away. Matt immediately noted he was Chinese and didn't seem to be armed.

The huge man, dressed in a long-sleeve shirt, jeans, and jogging shoes, raced with amazing speed directly toward him.

Matt quickly drew his Glock 19 and pointed it toward the charging Chinese giant.

"I've never seen such a mass of muscle," Ben said as he drew his pistol and pointed it at the charging giant.

Everyone else also drew their pistols and pointed them toward the Chinese giant, who was now approaching fast.

"Stop or we'll all start shooting," Matt yelled.

The Chinaman continued directly toward Matt.

"We should all open up and shoot him before he gets to us," Ben said He glanced at Matt.

The Chinaman kept his vigilant approach.

"You have one more chance to keep living," Matt yelled. "Stop immediately or we'll shoot."

The monster didn't stop.

Everyone started firing.

The monster kept coming.

Everyone continued firing.

The beast of a man slowed and staggered a little bit.

"Fire at his head," Matt yelled as he shifted his aim.

As they did, the monster dropped straight to the ground and lay still.

The only blood came from his head.

"He obviously has bullet-proof clothing," Matt said. "Even big slabs of tough muscle will bleed when hit with hi-caliber bullets."

Everyone nodded as they remained on alert and scanned the area.

"I'll check behind the bushes," Matt said. He held

his pistol in front of him and moved in that direction.

Another giant Chinaman came around the corner of the bushes with both hands held straight up.

"Hold your fire," Ben said. "It would be good to have a prisoner to interrogate. We might get some valuable information."

Ralph gave a short laugh. "Maybe, if we spoke Chinese."

"I'm sure we can find an interpreter if we can get him into custody," Ben said. He removed his phone and punched a button as the bull-like monster continued to move toward them with his hands in the air.

Justin and Vince also made calls.

Matt watched the man approach the group slowly. He noted the monster seemed to be coming more toward him.

The eight people all kept their pistols pointed at the intruder.

"A trained team is on the way, along with an appropriate vehicle to transport the monster," Ben said.

"Good," Matt replied as the bull-like monster drew closer.

Seeing a gleam in the bull's eyes, Matt figured he was going to be a target of the bull momentarily. He stayed on full alert and prepared for an attack. Recognizing the value of having a prisoner from Hugo Wagner's group, he exercised caution and refrained from shooting hastily.

The bull drew within five yards of Matt.

"Continue to hold your fire," Ben said. "Keep him covered but fire only on my command." He extended his pistol and pointed it toward the bull's head. "Hold it right there. You're close enough."

However, the bull didn't stop. He now moved directly toward Matt.

"If you don't stop, you're going to die like your partner," Ben yelled.

The bull ignored the command and continued straight toward his target.

Matt figured he needed to do something and not just stand there like a dummy. He had completed plenty of hand-to-hand training, some against huge men.

"Hold your fire for a minute," Matt yelled. He sprinted toward the bull and landed a vicious kick on his left knee.

The sudden move caught the bull by surprise.

Per his training, Matt put all of his strength and most of his 225 pounds of weight into it, but it didn't bring the bull down.

The blow only caused the bull to stumble slightly.

Matt pivoted quickly and gave him another strong kick to the right knee.

Despite the force behind the kick, there was no discernible impact or response.

Matt figured he wasn't going to be able to take this monster down and people would have to start shooting.

With surprising quickness, the bull planted his feet and launched a kick toward Matt's stomach.

Matt slid to his left with lightning speed, avoiding much of the blow.

However, the partial impact still inflicted some damage. Matt fought hard not to double over from the pain.

Matt figured Ben hadn't given the command to fire because there was too much risk someone would hit him instead of the bull. They had been shifting positions at high speed constantly and could do so again at any moment.

The monster glared at Matt. His blow had been delivered with enormous strength and he was looking more confident.

Matt could see concern on Ben's face as his finger tightened on the trigger of his Glock 19, but he didn't fire.

Matt kept his gaze focused on the monster and stayed fully ready for the next attack. He took a few steps back to try to increase the distance between them.

But the monster moved along with Matt and they stayed about three yards apart.

A grin now dominated the monster's face.

Matt stayed as prepared as he could for another attack.

With a menacing growl, the monster charged toward Matt. With a vicious swing, he aimed directly at Matt's head.

Matt ducked and put all of his strength into a kick, striking the bull's right knee.

Ignoring the kick, the bull pivoted toward Matt.

Matt darted to the side and made a quick turn away from the monster, but the monster followed.

"Fire!" Ben yelled.

A series of shots rang out.

The monster dropped onto the pavement, his body thrashing about until it finally lay still.

Matt started walking back toward the team.

In less than a minute, sirens blared as a procession of vehicles entered the parking lot and stopped.

A van designed to transport large prisoners was at the rear of the procession. A couple of unmarked cars were in the middle and some regular police cars with lights flashing had led the way into the area.

Matt saw Carl and George come out of the front of the building and walk toward them.

Several lawmen jumped out of the vehicles. Justin, Vince, and Ben walked toward some of them and engaged in a discussion as the other lawmen kept their weapons in ready position and searched the immediate area.

Carl and George walked over to the group around Matt.

"We heard all the gunshots and we immediately called the police," Carl said. "They told us they already knew about the situation and to stay inside. We had no idea what was going on. We heard all the sirens and got to a vantage point to see out and then we saw it was over."

George shrugged. "We won't ask you a lot of questions, but it looks like you were ambushed out here."

"Yep," Matt said. He pointed toward the hedge. "They were hidden over there. They were waiting for us to return to our vehicles."

One of the policemen walked over and took a long look at the assassin closest to them. He then glanced toward the other assassin. "The bastards must be close to seven feet tall and weigh over four hundred pounds." He turned back toward Matt and his group. "Glad you made it."

"Big guys all right, surprisingly agile too," Matt said.

Ben walked over to the group. "We shouldn't let our guard down," he said. "We need to stay alert. There could be a sniper around."

Everyone remained on alert.

"Let's wrap up here as quickly as possible and get back to our regular duties," Ben said. He looked at Ralph. "Have you finished making the enhancements to your security system at Tuxtun that we discussed?"

Ralph nodded. "They were completed late yesterday, as well as the ones to our homes. It should be more difficult for someone to break in and surprise us now."

"Good," Ben said. "The security enhancements to the FBI headquarters haven't been completed yet. We're waiting on some parts." He looked at Ralph. "If you agree, we'll meet over at Tuxtun to have our discussion about our current status and what action we'll take next."

Ralph gave a thumbs-up. "More than ever, we need to stay closely coordinated."

****

Hugo, Oleg, and Wan sat in their usual chairs in the center portion of the control room in their mountain fortress.

Hugo scowled and looked at Wan. "Well that didn't work out."

"They had some bad breaks," Wan said.

Hugo slammed his right fist on the desk. "They just didn't make the right decisions. They should have used their rifles. They could have targeted Baker and Gibson first and eliminated them for sure. Now we still have them around to deal with."

Oleg leaned toward Hugo. "Are you going to continue to spend time trying to kill Baker and Gibson?"

"Of course," Hugo said with a growl. "They must be eliminated. They're too much of a thorn in our side. We'll progress faster with our plans if they're completely out of our way."

"Are you going to use your expert German sniper you mentioned for your next attack?" Wan asked.

"Probably," Hugo said. "I'll decide in another day or two." He raised his right arm and made a dismissive gesture. "Maybe I've been concentrating on eliminating Baker and Gibson too much and taking time from other things we need to do. I'll definitely continue trying to get them out of our way but I'm going to take a break to concentrate on a couple of other important things, including destroying the Hidden Empire."

"Besides the Hidden Empire, what other things do you have in mind right now?" Oleg asked.

"Several things that will make a big difference in our progress for world domination," Hugo said. "First of all we lost all of our warehouses in the United States and we need to build some new ones." He focused his laser pointer on an image of a four-story building and another one under construction close by. "As we move forward with our plans we need some storage areas in the United States so we're constructing a warehouse next to the office building we built to help with our global finances. We own a large plot of land in the business park. The office building only takes up about a fourth of it."

Oleg and Wan nodded.

After Hugo manipulated several of the new displays, he focused the red dot from his laser pointer on one of the images.

The picture of what appeared to be a large ancient

castle loomed in front of the three men.

"What is that?" Oleg asked.

"One of the things I've been looking for," Hugo said. "This is one of the places some members of the Hidden Empire have been meeting."

"Are you sure about that?" Wan asked.

"I'm absolutely sure," Hugo said. "Some of my German engineers developed a research method designed to discover all the locations where the Hidden Empire conducts its strategy meetings. It has taken a while, but now they've found this one. It's a good start. We'll keep looking until we find all of them."

"Where is this one?" Oleg asked. He pointed toward the image of the ancient castle.

"About twenty miles east of Zurich, Switzerland," Hugo said. "I'm going to destroy it."

"They might have better defenses than we do. How do you plan to do that?" Wan asked.

Hugo looked at Oleg. "You just received a new stockpile of missiles from the Kremlin, didn't you?"

Oleg nodded. "They sent ten of each of the missiles I requested. The people I work with fully support our cause. They'll consider it a big victory for them if we can bring down the United States."

Hugo turned toward Wan. "We'll soon see how good their defenses are. We'll target this castle. It's easily within range of one of our tactical nukes. And we'll be using one of the latest models Russia sent us."

Wan nodded slowly.

"We need to remember the Russian KGB is probably the action arm for the Hidden Empire," Oleg said. "And I know for sure the KGB has unlimited access to all the Russian missiles."

"So you have some doubt about that?" Hugo asked.

Oleg wrinkled his brow, narrowed his eyes, and stared at Hugo. "About the Russian KGB being the action arm for the Hidden Empire?"

Hugo grunted and returned Oleg's stare. "That's what we're talking about, isn't it?"

"Why do you think I might have some doubt about that?"

"You said probably."

Oleg shrugged. "I've always heard that but it's hard to verify. Almost everything about the Hidden Empire is hard to verify."

"So if we target the Hidden Empire, we don't really know if the KGB might be a threat to us or not, right?" Hugo asked.

Oleg hesitated and then said, "Yeah, we don't really know, but if they are the action arm for the Hidden Empire they could possibly destroy us."

"Since the Kremlin supports what we're doing I would think the KGB would be reluctant to carry out a strike against us," Hugo said. He looked at Oleg and Wan. "Wouldn't both of you?"

Oleg again shrugged. "I have a lot of close friends in the Kremlin but I don't know anyone in the KGB very well. I guess it depends on where their loyalty lies."

Wan nodded. "It looks like we're in uncharted territory on this one."

"Well, first of all, I hope the KGB isn't really the action arm for the Hidden Empire," Hugo said. "And if by some chance they are, I hope they have as much loyalty to us as they do for the Hidden Empire."

"So you're thinking if they have loyalty to us they

probably wouldn't launch a strike against us even if the Hidden Empire asked them to?" Wan asked.

"That's exactly correct." Hugo raised his right fist straight up into the air. "I'm thinking we don't have to worry about a missile attack for several reasons. The first reason is that I'm convinced no one can determine our exact location. The second reason is that the Hidden Empire won't be able to launch one even if they know where we are. The third reason is that our defenses are good enough to repel any missile attack anyone launches against us."

Oleg and Wan didn't comment.

Hugo again focused his laser pointer on the image of the large ancient castle. "I'll do some more research and unless I find some reason not to, we'll go ahead and destroy the castle. It will send a strong message that we'll not tolerate being threatened by anyone, no matter how powerful they think they are. We'll strike back at anyone who tries to order us around." He slammed his right fist on the desktop again.

"I'm going to activate our plan to get the gold from the Federal Reserve Bank Depository in New York. We have the technology to hack into their system and create a lot of transactions for withdrawals by numerous legitimate depositors. I'll schedule a lot of shipments of the gold." Hugo laughed. "I'll schedule the gold to be shipped to the addresses of the depositors but I'll actually transport it over here to the large depository I've built."

"Oleg and I will make sure all the helicopters are fine-tuned and ready to use," Wan said.

"Do you still have Carmen and Hector in charge of that?" Hugo asked.

"That hasn't changed," Wan said.

"Are they still in Mexico and do you still coordinate with them every day?" Hugo asked.

"Everything is running the same way as it did when I first set it up," Wan said. "They keep the helicopters at a secluded airfield close to them and they make sure the right people in the Mexican Government receive their money on time every month."

"I haven't thought about Carmen and Hector much after that stupid debacle with the bazooka," Hugo said. "But it's good you're keeping up with them and the helicopters. We certainly need to keep the helicopters on that side of the Atlantic Ocean for now. That's where we're going to use them first."

Wan regarded Hugo carefully. "Oleg and I both check with them often. They assure us they talk to the pilots and maintenance personnel every day. They even conduct an inspection of the facility every week to make sure every helicopter is ready to use when needed."

Hugo narrowed his eyes slightly as he looked at Wan and Oleg. "I want both of you to double-check everything and make sure all the helicopters are fine-tuned and ready to use. And make sure you tell Carman and Hector to keep all the helicopters ready to go on a moment's notice."

Wan and Oleg both nodded.

"Are you still planning to get the gold from the United States Mint locations also?" Oleg asked.

"That's going to be a little more difficult," Hugo said. "They don't do a lot of pickups and deliveries like the Federal Reserve with their multitude of foreign accounts." He looked at Wan. "Let's see how it goes with the Federal Reserve and then we'll work out a plan to get the gold from the Mint locations. We'll plan to do Fort Knox first. That's where they have the most gold stored."

"It might also be a lot more secure than their other locations," Oleg said. He stared at Hugo for a moment.

Hugo shrugged. "With our capability we'll figure out a way to disable all their security systems and then we'll devise a great plan to get the gold."

****

Late the next morning in Jacksonville, Matt, Ralph, Todd, Judy, and Steve sat at the large table in the main conference room at Tuxtun with Ben, Justin, and Vince.

"Quite an adventure yesterday but I'm glad we got the tour completed at the University of Florida," Ben said. "We know Hugo Wagner is going to continue to hack into the Federal Reserve System and it's good to know there's some defense for that in place."

Todd nodded. "Judy and I think he'll use his quantum computer to go after the gold too. We think he'll set up fake transactions for shipping the gold back to the depositors but actually ship the gold to himself."

"How did you come up with that?" Ben asked.

"Judy and I connected some pieces of this giant puzzle we're working on." Todd gave a short laugh. "I guess we put two and two together, so to speak."

Judy nodded. "We know Wagner has a quantum computer and has been hacking into various less powerful computers. Carl and George mentioned the main computer at the Federal Reserve has already fought off some hacking attempts, thanks to their help."

"It's good they were able to develop a quantum computer to play defense," Todd said.

"We know Wagner is going after the gold supply and we know he has a fleet of helicopters to transport the gold." Judy scanned the faces around her. "Todd and I did several hours of analysis this morning and we think we've deducted one of the things Wagner is going to be concentrating on in the very near future." She held both arms out with her palms up. "At least that's our best guess."

"I can't argue with your logic," Matt said.

Ben grunted. "It's difficult to decide where to start the conversation. I received a lot more intelligence information last night. We have a lot to talk about. Is everyone familiar with IAPRA?"

"I think some of us might need some explanation." Steve looked at Ben. "I know I do."

"IAPRA stands for Intelligence Advanced Research Projects Activity," Ben said. And while we're on the subject, HSARPA stands for Homeland Security Advanced Research Projects Agency, and DARPA stands for Defense Advanced Research Projects Agency. I just got security updates from all of them."

Steve gave a slow nod.

"IARPA does a lot of research on quantum computing." Ben looked at Todd and Judy. "I'm glad you went first. The new information they sent me ties into what you said. HSARPA and DARPA also sent updates that tie into what you told us. I think we can be assured Hugo Wagner is going to go after at least some of the gold real soon."

Ben took several minutes to explain various aspects of the new information.

"So where does this new information leave us in the grand scheme of things?" Ralph asked.

"We know Hugo Wagner is greedy, he holds grudges, and he wants to conquer the world, among other things." Matt studied the faces around him. "And I'm sure one of his foremost objectives continues to be killing all of us, especially Ralph and me."

"Whatever we do we had better keep what Matt just mentioned in mind as we go forward," Ralph said.

Everyone nodded.

"We all want to go on living while we're trying to solve this maze of problems we're dealing with." Ben looked directly at Matt. "We're all in this together and we all know we must eliminate Wagner and his operation before we can breathe easily again." Ben glanced at Ralph. "To answer the question you posed a little bit ago, I think this new information I received leaves us in a more knowledgeable position to make some rapid progress on several issues. We need to set some priorities."

Matt leaned toward Ben. "Was there any new information relating to the Hidden Empire in what you received?"

"Some," Ben said. "We'll talk about it. Hopefully, by the time we finish our discussion, we'll have a better grasp on how to develop a solution to many aspects of this."

"We're dealing with two immensely powerful groups who're involved in this situation," Justin said. "This whole thing has gotten so complex it's going to be difficult to tie together all the loose ends so we know exactly what's going on."

"Right," Vince said. "Lot of pieces to the puzzle. We haven't heard from Carmen Vargas and Hector Medina in a while and they're probably still around."

Ben nodded. "We have quite a bit of intelligence on them. They're still in Mexico and they're in charge of getting Hugo's helicopters ready to carry a lot of gold. I just got that information too. It looks like several things are getting ready to explode."

"Have you discovered their exact location in Mexico yet?" Matt asked.

Ben nodded. "They're both in Mexico City. With all their money, you would expect them to be well off, and they are. Each has a big mansion in the most affluent area of the city."

"Do you think we'll have any more personal threats from them anytime soon?" Ralph asked.

"There was nothing specific about that in the latest intelligence I received. We'll keep them under surveillance and see how it plays out." Ben shook his head. "This whole thing is not only convoluted logic-wise, it's also a big political mess. Along with Hugo Wagner's group and the Hidden Empire, Russia and China are big concerns. There also are people in Mexico, Cuba, and Germany involved in this in some way. When you look at all the tangle of money flow, you can also add in a lot of small countries along with some more large ones such as Syria and Saudi Arabia from the Middle East."

"I used to think the Saudis were our friends," Ralph said, "but lately it seems it's not turning out that way."

"Some Saudis still are." Ben narrowed his eyes. "This whole thing is getting more complicated every day. Many of our experts think some of what's going on might even trigger another world war."

"So what's the bottom line after the recent events?"

Matt asked.

"Hard to define," Ben said. "There's a huge amount of international oil money involved in all this. There's a lot of collusion among a lot of diverse entities. Drug cartels in Cuba and Mexico have hooked up with oil cartels. The Russians are supplying nukes to multiple entities. We think Hugo Wagner and the Hidden Empire are among them."

"How did we find out about the Hidden Empire receiving a nuke?" Justin asked.

"That's a really long story and it's classified," Ben said. "However, I can assure you it's true. A tactical nuke was just delivered this morning to a location in Switzerland that we've found to be a functional part of the Hidden Empire."

There was a brief silence.

"Getting back to how convoluted this mess we're dealing with is," Ben said. "All the international financial institutions, the World Bank, the IMF, and the WTO among them, are facilitating the money flow."

"What's the latest intelligence regarding the role of the Federal Reserve?" Ralph asked.

"We're sure some people there are directly involved in this whole activity regarding the global money flow," Ben said, "but we can't prove it yet." His gaze focused on Ralph and Matt. "Many of the financial analysts in the FBI and CIA are still spending full time on this. I hope you'll continue to keep Judy and Todd heavily involved with them."

"That's our intention," Ralph said.

Matt nodded.

"Do you have something specific you want Ralph and me to do next?" Matt asked.

"Sit tight for a while," Ben said. "The right path of action should present itself soon. I've sent queries to a lot of people who can supply some needed information. I'll review what they say and get back to you."

Ralph and Matt both nodded.

"Is the situation with Cuba still about missile placements?" Matt asked.

"Yes," Ben said. "And we still don't know who's behind the activity. We've uncovered a lot of the money flow to Cuban leaders, but we still haven't been able to trace any of it all the way back to its origin."

"So we don't know if it's Hugo Wagner or someone else?" Vince asked.

"That's correct," Ben said. "We think the missile placements in Cuba are all connected to Hugo Wagner, but we're not absolutely sure yet. Along with the mountain of other things, we'll continue to work on it."

Judy nodded. "Todd and I have been helping with that and we think we're making some progress, but no definitive conclusions yet."

Ben leaned forward. "I'm glad you're making some progress. It's certainly one hell of a puzzle."

Matt didn't comment. He regretted not having specific knowledge of some details that could be a big help in the analysis.

"We'll stay on full alert and use every aspect of our surveillance capability while we're trying to figure things out," Ben said.

"Meaning NRO and NSA?" Matt asked.

"We'll use different capabilities of all our other intelligence services too." Ben said. "They all have things they can contribute. Whoever has started to set up the missile sites in Cuba wouldn't do that if they didn't plan to use them. Our military will get involved as soon as any missiles show up. I hope we can determine exactly what they plan to do before it's too late."

Matt leaned forward. "Like you mentioned, the whole situation is a convoluted mess. We have our work cut out for us."

"When I get the feedback from the queries I sent out, I'll get back to everybody and we'll all get busy again," Ben said. He made a dismissive gesture. "In the meantime, we can all benefit from a short break in the action."

Ben, Justin, and Vince stood to leave.

Matt felt grateful he and Ralph were getting a short break.

Chapter 23

In his luxury mansion in Mexico City, Hector looked across the round conference table in his office at Carmen.

"Thanks for driving over," Hector said. "I still think it's best we don't discuss our plans over the phone."

Carmen nodded. "Even though Hugo and his group constantly tell us we have a completely secure communications system, I figure the Hidden Empire probably has access to all of our phone conversations."

Hector gave a slight shrug. "I don't know if we're under surveillance or not, but it's always safer to have important discussions face-to-face."

"I completely agree. If we constantly sweep our homes for bugs, this is the most secure way to have a conversation." Carmen narrowed his eyes and leaned toward Hector. "And speaking of that, have you just swept for bugs over here?"

"Yes, I have my security team do that four times a day." Hector looked at his watch. "They completed a sweep thirty minutes ago."

"Well, let's get to the business at hand." Carmen took a deep breath, exhaled slowly, and leaned forward. "I'm assuming you received a phone call from Wan like I did this morning?"

Hector nodded.

"And I'm sure he gave you a heads-up that Hugo is about ready to start getting the gold, right?" Carmen asked.

"Right, and I told him we were both sitting on ready."

"Do they have their plan all worked out?"

"I asked him about that, didn't you?"

"What did he tell you?"

"That they were still working out some details but we should stay ready to go on a moment's notice."

"He told me the same thing. Just want to make sure before we got very far along on our discussion."

"Did Wan have any specific suggestions on any readiness procedures?"

"He didn't mention any to me." Carmen looked expectantly at Hector.

"Same here," Hector said.

Carmen gave a slight shrug. "I guess we'll just keep doing what we've been doing."

"Yeah," Hector said as he leaned slightly toward Carmen. "Did he mention Hugo's plans for another assassination attempt?"

"Against Baker and Gibson?"

Hector nodded.

Carmen wrinkled his brow. "I had a long conversation with him about the helicopters but that subject never came up."

"What time did he call you?"

"Early this morning," Hector said. He hesitated a moment. "It was about eight o'clock our time."

"He didn't call me until about noon. I guess he had new information from Hugo and any assassination plans are on hold."

"I think Hugo's down to just one assassin now and he's German."

"Maybe they'll want us to provide some more Hispanic assassins?"

"We probably should start preparing for that."

Carmen nodded and said, "As long as it doesn't interfere with being prepared to go get the gold."

****

In an elaborate castle in Switzerland about twenty miles east of Zurich, Vulcan sat in his usual chair in a plush lounge area.

Neptune and Apollo occupied two other chairs in the lounge. Vulcan had sent them an urgent message two hours ago that he had some new items to discuss.

Apollo watched patiently as both Vulcan and Neptune reached for their pipes, tobacco, and lighters. He was used to their mannerisms by now.

"Zeus sent me a message that he was going to meet us here at some point to discuss an important subject," Vulcan said. "But he wanted me to meet with you first and bring you up to date on what's going on."

Neptune nodded slowly and didn't comment.

"Did Zeus give you any information about what the subject was?" Apollo asked.

"I'll get to that in just a minute," Vulcan said. "It requires a little discussion. I'll bring you up to date on some things before he has his meeting with us to make sure we all have a full understanding of what needs to be done."

Neptune and Apollo didn't comment.

Vulcan started methodically filling his pipe with his favorite almond-blend tobacco.

He waited until Neptune also filled his pipe.

201

From past experience, Apollo knew it was cherry-blend tobacco.

Apollo figured if he ever started smoking he would choose a pipe and the cherry-flavored tobacco that Neptune used. The cherry flavor appealed to him much more than the apple flavor that Vulcan preferred.

Neptune flicked his lighter and positioned the flame. While taking a few puffs to get his pipe going, he glanced toward their elder leader, Vulcan.

Vulcan slowly adjusted his position and looked at the other two men.

"It's now certain Hugo Wagner will continue to interfere with the global money flow in several ways, even though he's been warned twice," Vulcan said. "Zeus has informed me Hugo will be eliminated and his entire operation destroyed."

"When?" Apollo asked.

Neptune slowly took a large puff from his pipe and fixed his gaze on Vulcan. "How soon will that happen?"

"Hopefully before Hugo shoots a missile at us," Vulcan said. "Zeus told me Hugo has discovered the location of this castle and was making preparations to destroy it."

Apollo leaned toward Vulcan with a questioning expression on his face. "I assume Hugo is still going after the gold supply?"

Vulcan nodded. "Zeus told me Hugo was concentrating on the Federal Reserve supply in New York first."

"Do the three of us need to do something specific about any of these things?" Apollo asked.

"Zeus told me he was taking care of everything and

he would give us a full explanation of the details shortly when he meets with us."

Neptune took a long puff on his pipe and then asked, "Is the meeting going to be here?"

"I don't know," Vulcan said.

"Apollo narrowed his eyes. "Didn't you ask him?"

"No, he was in a big hurry. I'm sure he'll give us all the necessary details when he schedules the meeting." Vulcan's gaze took in both Apollo and Neptune as he took a puff on his pipe.

"So Zeus doesn't want us to take any action?" Apollo asked.

"Certainly not at this time," Vulcan said. "Like I mentioned, he's making sure everything is being taken care of and he'll give us the details when he meets with us."

Apollo pressed his lips together and waited. Sometimes he found his partners' mannerisms a little irritating, like now. He liked to get all the important information quicker, not have it dribble out a little at a time.

"If Hugo is able to steal all five thousand tons of gold from the Federal Reserve Bank of New York, he'll definitely have an immediate negative effect on the global money flow." Neptune shook his head slowly.

Vulcan nodded. "Taking all that gold out of the global monetary system would certainly change things for us and we can't let that happen. Zeus will make sure we take the necessary actions to prevent Hugo from doing that."

"I'm still worried about this," Apollo said. "We know Hugo has a very secure setup. Even though we know his location, we might not be able to stop him."

Vulcan leaned forward. "We have super-advanced technology too. I'm confident we'll stop him."

"I hope Zeus meets with us real soon," Apollo said. "I'm eager to gather more specifics and anxious to get away from this location. I'm guessing we don't yet know how quickly Hugo is going to fire his missile?"

Vulcan narrowed his eyes. "We have to trust Zeus, Jupiter, and Odin to do the right things."

****

At their fortress in southern Germany, Hugo Wagner, Oleg Titov, and Wan Lu sat in their usual chairs in their hi-tech control room.

Hugo scanned the multiple displays on the circular wall and focused his laser pointer on a specific image of an ancient castle.

Both Oleg and Wan studied the information around the area of the red dot and waited for Hugo to comment.

Hugo looked at Oleg. "Do we have the correct missile in place?"

"Two of them. Thought you might want to use both. We don't know how good their anti-missile defense might be," Oleg said. "I thought you might want some extra insurance."

"Yeah, it's probably good to have some backup." Hugo shrugged. "Like you say, we don't know how good their anti-missile defense is."

"The two missiles we have in place each have a blast radius of one-half mile," Oleg said. "We can aim them at precisely the same spot or we can spread out the landing spots a little bit."

Hugo nodded but remained quiet.

"Also, we can fire them at the same time or we can stagger the firing times," Oleg said. "We want to be sure we get the job done."

Hugo looked at Wan. "You're our best strategist. What do you consider to be our optimal strategy?"

"I know you always think it will be good to have overwhelming odds for accomplishing anything we do," Wan said. "Give me a few moments to think about it." He issued some verbal commands to their control system and instantly looked at a large display of information.

Oleg narrowed his eyes as he turned toward Hugo. "I worked with one of our teams on developing our tactical nukes. I also have some thoughts about what our optimal strategy should be."

Hugo gave a quick nod and then glanced at Wan. "Let us know when you've formed an opinion and we'll discuss it."

"Of course," Wan said. "It will be good to make sure we consider all the variables. We don't want to overlook anything."

Hugo nodded and smiled as he and Oleg also studied the information Wan had on display.

Five minutes later, Wan completed his research. He stopped and looked at Hugo and Oleg. He waited for each of them to get to a stopping point in their reading and look back at him before he spoke.

"Well, I have an opinion and it's based on a thorough review of the situation," Wan said.

Hugo nodded. "Let's have it."

"I think we should fire both missiles at the same spot but we should have a ten-second interval between them," Wan said. "If the Hidden Empire has a good missile defense system in place, two consecutive missiles close together might overwhelm it."

Oleg nodded. "That's my thinking exactly."

"How soon do you want to fire the missiles?" Wan asked.

"Three people just left the castle. We'll wait until they have their next meeting." Hugo gestured toward one of the images. "It will be a bigger blow to them if we eliminate some of their leaders along with their castle."

Wan and Oleg nodded.

"Okay, we have a plan for the missiles," Hugo said. "We'll get back to work on deactivating specific security features at the Federal Reserve Bank of New York so we can get the gold."

Wan leaned toward Hugo. "I think Oleg and I have most of it figured out. We can alert Carmen and Hector to make plans for the helicopters to be in New York tomorrow afternoon at five o'clock Eastern Standard Time."

Hugo made a circular gesture covering the room. "Okay, we'll make a final check on everything and then we'll notify them."

"We're still planning to get all the gold quickly and use the whole fleet of helicopters, right?" Oleg asked.

"Right," Hugo said. "We have our own state-of-the-art helicopter carrier sitting out in the Atlantic ready to refuel them." He laughed. "With our money, we have a tremendous capability and it's getting better all the time. We have three more carriers ready now for later exploits. We have another one in the Atlantic and two in the Pacific. In addition to having more capability for transporting gold all over the world, we're soon going to be able to launch some very surprising attacks on several countries."

Wan gave a short laugh. "And with five thousand more tons of gold, we can keep up our rate of spending for a long time."

Hugo again made a sweeping gesture at the various displays on the screen. "With the power of our quantum computer, I'm sure we can continue all of our plans to our satisfaction." He looked at Wan. "Carmen and Hector are probably together. Call Carmen right now and tell both of them to get ready to do their thing tomorrow afternoon. We'll go ahead and get the gold as our next step and then we'll concentrate on teaching the Hidden Empire to not mess with us. They need to recognize we're more powerful than they are."

Wan nodded and reached for his phone.

Chapter 24

In his luxury mansion in Mexico City, Carmen picked up his vibrating phone and answered. From the display, he knew Wan was calling.

"I just checked a lot of things and made sure we had a secure connection," Wan said. "You can talk freely."

"Okay, so are you ready to use the helicopters?" Carmen asked.

"Do you have your phone on speaker?"

"Yes, and we're in a secluded sound-proofed room in the house."

"Good, Hector needs to hear all the conversation."

"He's listening."

"Yes, we're ready to use the helicopters and the big question is if you have them ready to use," Wan said.

"You're damned right we're ready, and we've been ready for a good while now."

"Can the whole fleet be at the Federal Reserve Bank in New York tomorrow afternoon to load the gold?"

"Of course, what time?"

"Five o'clock Eastern Time."

"We'll be there."

"Good, we already have your route mapped out and downloaded to every helicopter."

"Do we have enough capacity on the choppers to

carry all the gold being withdrawn?"

"We've calculated every detail several times in the last two weeks. You have enough capacity."

Carmen didn't say anything as he waited for Wan to continue.

"The plan we provided instructed to stagger your flights, ensuring that the sky isn't overcrowded with helicopters. That would attract a lot of attention on the ground."

"We'll conform strictly to the plan. They'll go on a multitude of different routes and in small groups."

"We've carefully planned the gold pickups so no more than two helicopters are coming into the loading area together," Wan said. He went on to explain more details.

"So you have a helicopter carrier sitting out in the Atlantic right now?" Carmen asked.

"It's at the exact location it needs to be to refuel the fleet for coming over here. All that information is programmed into each helicopter's navigation system."

Carmen pursed his lips and nodded. He stared at Hector, who gave a thumbs-up.

"If some of your calculations don't work out right or if some of the choppers have mechanical problems, have you done anything to ensure we'll continue to have enough helicopter capacity to transport all the gold?" Carmen asked.

"We have some extra helicopters on the carrier. If we need them we'll send them to make sure we carry all the gold. They're fully programmed and they'll operate on the same principles you're using. They'll spread out around the metropolitan area to provide any assistance needed."

Carmen and Hector listened to a few more details before Wan concluded.

After Wan disconnected, Carmen looked at Hector. "Do you think it will work okay?"

Hector nodded. "It sounds like an excellent plan to me."

****

The next morning at the Jacksonville FBI Headquarters, Matt, Ralph, Justin, Vince, Judy, Todd, and Steve sat with Ben at the large table in the main conference room.

"I got a lot of feedback from the queries I sent out. We're dealing with one hell of a situation," Ben said, "and we've now thrown all of our intelligence resources into the fight."

Matt narrowed his eyes. "I thought they were all involved a long time ago. This has been a convoluted mess for a long time."

Ralph nodded.

"We actually weren't using all of them, but we're now making use of every available intelligence resource that can benefit us," Ben explained. "And many of our analysts are now working closely with several think tanks. RAND is one of them."

Matt knew RAND was founded in 1948 to help the U.S. Air Force prepare for World War III and it had evolved into an organization that dealt with many intricate societal problems in addition to those assigned to it by the government and the military. He knew it still had a strong focus on acquiring and analyzing information pertaining to national security.

"The threat matrix has been all over the place the last few weeks," Ben said, "We've been dealing with a lot of the threats and there are a lot more to deal with."

Matt wondered where Ben was headed with this, but he refrained from asking any questions at this point.

"The consensus from the think tanks is that Hugo Wagner and the Hidden Empire now are enemies," Ben said. "Each one is planning to destroy the other one."

Matt furrowed a brow. "I thought the Hidden Empire supported what Hugo was doing."

"They did for a while," Ben said. "It seems the Hidden Empire liked the disruption Hugo was causing but that has changed. Hugo crossed the line by planning to grab all the gold stored at the Federal Reserve and the U.S. Mint. Hugo's grabbing the gold will cause changes to the global money flow that will negatively affect the Hidden Empire."

Judy nodded. "Todd and I have been working with RAND on that issue. RAND concluded that if Hugo does that, it will cut off a way that the Hidden Empire gets a significant amount of their funding."

"How did RAND come to that conclusion?" Ralph asked.

"It's complicated and I'm not sure Judy and I can explain all the details properly," Todd said.

Ben leaned forward. "Give us a summary."

"RAND uses a sophisticated version of game theory," Todd said. "They're applying probabilistic mathematics to determine the most likely explanation for certain things. They're trying to predict the most probable enemy actions based on their latest threats. They've determined Hugo and his group want to keep us off balance and then destroy us."

"Yeah, it seems the Hidden Empire liked Hugo's use of misdirection and deception to create a lot of disruption for a while," Ben said. "But it looks like Hugo is now planning to do some things that negatively affect them. They won't tolerate it."

Judy nodded. "Experts at RAND are convinced both Hugo and the Hidden Empire have a complicated plan in motion."

"Each one is planning to destroy the other, right?" Matt asked.

"Based on all the feedback I just received, that seems to be the case," Ben said. "There are a lot of details we haven't covered but I think our intelligence agencies know enough at this stage to help us prepare to take the action we need to take."

A brief silence ensued.

Ben looked at Todd. "Go ahead and mention the bit about the four republics you and Judy uncovered in your research with RAND."

"We came across a prediction the United States will be broken up into four republics controlled by China, Canada, the European Union, and Mexico," Todd said. "Some mention was made about Russia wanting a part too. I'm not sure how that would be worked out."

"What about Hugo? Doesn't he want the whole thing?" Matt asked.

Todd gave a short laugh. "Yeah, we're pretty sure he still wants all of it. I think China and Russia each want all of it too. They all seem to be cooperating right now. Maybe they're planning to end up being partners in some way."

Ben continued the discussion for another hour and then scanned the faces around him. "We need to decide what our specific group is going to do next. But before we do that, I have something to show you."

He stood and gestured for everyone to follow him.

Ben led everyone into a large room with a multitude of computer screens on a wall.

Everyone sat on one side of a long table stretching across a large area in the middle of the room. They all faced the screens.

Ben explained this was a new operations center designed to facilitate their ability to make progress on all the new issues. He punched a button on a small device in front of him. One of the screens on the wall came alive and displayed a truck carrying a load of large metal barrels.

"Each of these containers has a different type of biochemical. They were unloaded on the docks at JAXPORT last night," Ben said.

"How did you get this information?" Ralph asked.

Ben gestured toward the row of screens. "We have an improved intelligence system and we now have better access to all the available information. The details are top secret and I'll leave it at that."

Matt narrowed his eyes. "So back to the biochemical containers, we have more to worry about than just the nukes."

Ben nodded as he hit some more buttons on his control device.

A close-up image of the barrels appeared on the screen.

"And note, these are all unmarked containers," Ben said. "We figure Hugo is behind this but we haven't verified that yet. Our analysts are working on tracing various things back to the source but they're having some trouble." He looked at Todd and Judy. "You've been working with our FBI analysts on a lot of these issues, thought you might want to make some comments."

"Among other things, we're trying to follow the money and we're still trying to unravel the financial maze," Judy said. "We've known from the beginning that Hugo and his group are very smart people and it's no surprise they have the money flow so tangled up it's almost undetectable. However, we're making some progress. We'll keep everyone posted on the progress and maybe we can all tie some more significant items together real soon."

"What about the Hidden Empire, any progress on that?" Matt asked.

Judy gave a short laugh. "As usual, they skillfully stay well hidden but we're sure they're involved in some aspects of what we're dealing with. We still think the Illuminati functions as their action arm and the Russian KGB functions as their hit squad when needed."

"I doubt the Hidden Empire has any connection to these barrels of biochemical liquid," Ben said. "It's likely they're intended to be converted into biochemical weapons. I'm sure Hugo is behind this. We think he might decide to target the area around Cape Canaveral. That's why we had our tour down there to be familiar with the area, in case we're needed in some way." He pressed some more buttons on his control device.

A long-range image of the industrial park where the new international finance office was located appeared.

Ben zoomed in on the image.

An office building and what was obviously a

warehouse appeared.

"They haven't tried to resume financial operations in the office building, but they've added a warehouse since our visit," Ben said. "And we think that's where the truck with the chemicals is going. It should be no surprise to us that things are still escalating."

Matt grunted. "No kidding."

Some people chuckled. Matt figured everyone was trying to stay loose. He knew they all were aware they functioned a lot better when they didn't get too uptight.

"Well, returning to the serious side of things, it looks that there will soon be a stash of biochemical weapons at that warehouse," Ben said. "I think we need to pay them a visit."

"Why don't you just send in a large, well-equipped SWAT team?" Vince asked. "Justin and I can both supply the necessary manpower."

"That's an option we'll keep in mind as we go forward. And don't forget about Carmen Vargas and Hector Medina," Ben said. "They're still around. NSA has intercepted several phone calls from them in the last few days. They probably think they have a secure communications setup but NSA has made some significant enhancements lately."

"Are they both in Mexico City?" Matt asked.

Ben nodded. "And we know they're still working with Hugo Wagner and his group."

"Does that have any connection to what we need to do at the warehouse?" Vince asked.

"My bosses in Washington think there might be a lot of things going on at the warehouse," Ben said. "They think there might be a lot of illegal drugs stored there, along with some missiles. They think Carmen and Hector will visit to check on the illegal drugs."

"Do your bosses think Vargas and Medina might be making a trip there soon?" Matt asked.

"You got it," Ben said. "After NSA decrypted a lot of the phone conversations, my bosses think Carmen and Hector are using the warehouse as part of their drug trafficking scheme. They'll likely show up there soon to check the storage of the drugs."

"We think the chemicals are going there but do we think any missiles are going there, or perhaps are already there?" Matt asked.

"Some tactical nukes and other types of missiles are already there," Ben said. "And we know for sure. Hugo has been threatening to use missiles against us. We know a lot about what's going on as well as a lot about the people involved. We've also proven we're very capable of doing our work. I think that's a likely reason why my bosses will want our specific group to inspect the warehouse. We've been successful on everything so far."

****

The next morning in Switzerland, three elder men each sat in his favorite cushioned chair in a plush lounge area in the ancient castle twenty miles from Zurich.

"Zeus just sent notice he has completed a long discussion with Jupiter, and Odin," Vulcan said. "Everything is now sitting on go to destroy Hugo and his group."

"Do we have a specific time yet as to when this will happen?" Neptune asked.

Apollo rubbed his chin but didn't comment.

Vulcan took a moment to light his pipe and take a

puff. Neptune also lit his pipe and took a puff of his favorite cherry-blend tobacco.

"Zeus will meet with us tomorrow and give us all the details," Vulcan said. "He also mentioned he's going to go over some of our history that he wants to be sure we know."

"Is he coming here?" Apollo asked.

"No," Vulcan said. "He told me it would be too dangerous. Hugo is planning to hit this castle with a tactical nuke and destroy it as well as everything within a half-mile radius around it."

"Does Zeus know if we're safe at the moment?" Neptune asked.

"I asked him that question," Vulcan said. "He told me they had a way to keep up with everything Hugo was doing. We have at least another day before we need to worry about a missile strike." He took another puff from his pipe.

Neptune and Apollo anxiously leaned toward Vulcan.

"Zeus said Hugo wouldn't be able to launch his missile against us until tomorrow at the earliest," Vulcan said. He noted both Apollo and Neptune exhaled sharply and looked relieved.

"So where are we going to meet?" Apollo asked.

"Zeus didn't tell me," Vulcan said, "but he mentioned the three of us would receive a message here a little later in the morning that would give us all the necessary instructions."

"We know Hugo has a very secure setup and he possibly has the best technology on the planet," Neptune said. "I still think there's a chance we might not be able to stop him."

Apollo narrowed his eyes. "I agree with Neptune. I also think that's still an issue for us."

Neptune and Apollo both looked directly at Vulcan.

"Zeus affirmed we have better technology than Hugo does. Remember, we know exactly where he is, and we have a lot of options," Vulcan said. "Zeus gave me his assurance we have a lot of capability Hugo doesn't know about and we're prepared to use all of it."

"Did he give you any information about that capability?" Apollo asked.

Vulcan nodded. "He mentioned we have direct access to a large fully functional missile system with super advanced technology along with advanced support systems."

There was a brief silence.

"Zeus assured me we'll wipe Hugo off the face of the earth and be done with it," Vulcan said. "We won't have to be concerned about him creating severe problems for us anymore."

Vulcan glanced at his watch. "We should be getting a message about our next meeting with Zeus any minute now."

Chapter 25

In southern Germany, Hugo Wagner, Oleg Titov, and Wan Lu sat in their usual chairs in the middle of the hi-tech control room at their fortress.

Lucas Becker, the other German assassin Hugo had available, sat in the fourth chair.

Hugo glanced at Lucas. "You know you're going after Baker and Gibson, and you know a lot about the situation from the briefings you've already received. I thought it would be good for you to join us and get more thoroughly briefed on all the details of your mission. You'll be a lot more aware of some key details that could be important. This time we *must* succeed."

"And my next mission is in Jacksonville, Florida, right?" Lucas asked.

"That's correct," Hugo said. He scanned the multiple displays on the circular wall and focused his laser pointer on an image showing an expanded view of a specific area.

"This is the industrial park south of Jacksonville," Hugo said. "You'll be leaving for there in a few minutes. One of our high-speed jets will get you there quickly." He turned and looked directly at Lucas.

Lucas nodded and didn't comment.

Hugo zoomed in on the image. Two buildings were now on display. One was the four-story office building originally constructed for the international finance group to use. The other building was a large two-story warehouse. The gray exterior walls of both buildings were made of massive stone blocks. He focused the red dot on the warehouse and then punched some other buttons on his control device. A video appeared on one display and gave a slow tour of the inside of the warehouse.

In a few minutes, Hugo stopped the video and punched some more buttons on his control device.

An image showing a view of an aisle with rows of wooden crates on each side appeared and the image of a floor plan appeared beside it.

Hugo then focused on some information appearing on another display.

Oleg, Wan, and Lucas all studied the information around the area of the red dot and waited for Hugo to comment.

Hugo looked at Lucas. "Have you finished reading all the information?"

Lucas gestured toward the image of the floor plan. "Is that the first or second floor?"

"It's the first floor. The second has an entirely different layout," Hugo said. "You can choose which floor you set up in when you get a chance to look everything over after you get there."

Lucas nodded. "Yes, I've read all the information. The first floor will probably be my choice. I've picked the exact spot where I need to set up and I know the surrounding layout."

"Do you have any more questions?" Hugo asked.

Lucas kept his gaze focused on the display and shook his head slowly. "No, I think everything is clear."

Hugo turned toward Oleg. "So you'll be ready to

fire two missiles at the castle tomorrow from our launch system here?"

Oleg gave a thumbs-up. "Since we don't yet know how good their anti-missile defense is, we'll plan to add some extra insurance." He gave a quick explanation. "We should be ready to fire before noon tomorrow."

"And the two missiles we have in place each have a blast radius of one-half mile?" Hugo asked.

"Right, and they're both aimed at precisely the same spot," Oleg said. He again gave a thumbs-up.

Hugo nodded and looked at Wan. "Did you and Oleg set every detail up exactly like we discussed?"

"The plan is the same except I recommend we have a fifteen-second interval instead of a ten-second interval between firing the missiles," Wan said.

Hugo leaned slightly toward Wan. "Why the change?"

"You left me in charge of the launch strategy and I had another discussion with all of our analysts. I'm a dedicated perfectionist," Wan said. "We decided that a slightly longer interval between the launches will be more effective. The explanation is complicated but we think we've improved our probability of getting the results we want." He looked directly at Hugo. "In case the Hidden Empire does indeed have a good missile defense system in place, we think our new timing on the two consecutive missiles close together will have a better chance to overwhelm it."

Hugo nodded slowly. "I hope you're right."

Hugo looked over at Lucas. "We'll take care of things on this side of the Atlantic while you take care of things on the other side."

Lucas nodded.

"As far as perfecting plans go, I've just decided to have a couple of people join you in the warehouse. Carmen Vargas and Hector Medina are two drug lords we work with and they're good with weapons."

Lucas stared curiously at Hugo.

"They're storing a lot of drugs in the warehouse to facilitate their drug trafficking," Hugo said. "And I'm also storing some missiles and some bio-chemical weapons in there. Carmen and Hector have already planned a trip over to check some things. I'll also ask them to give you some added support in killing Baker, Gibson, and whoever else is with them."

"How good with weapons are they?" Lucas asked.

"They've had a lot of skirmishes with rival drug cartels and they're still alive," Hugo said. "That alone speaks volumes."

"Where are they now?" Lucas asked.

"In Mexico City," Hugo said. "But they can travel fast. They have a fleet of private jets."

Lucas nodded slowly and didn't comment.

"What weapons are you carrying now?" Hugo asked.

"I carry a SIG 556 rifle and a Heckler & Koch USP pistol," Lucas said. "The SIG 556 uses NATO 5.56mm rounds and can fire 900 rounds per minute. It has a thirty-round magazine."

Hugo gave a short laugh. "Sounds like you know your equipment well."

"In my profession, it helps to be a perfectionist." Lucas looked directly at Hugo. "The magazine in my Heckler & Koch USP pistol holds fifteen 9x19 mm Parabellum cartridges. I'll have plenty of firepower."

"That's good," Hugo said as he glanced at Wan.

"As soon as Lucas gets on his way, go ahead and give Carmen another call. He and Hector need to be in Jacksonville in a few hours. We know Baker is going to be in a group making a surprise raid on the warehouse later this morning their time."

"How do you know the time?" Lucas asked.

Hugo made a circular gesture at all the displayed information. "We have many ways of collecting our information."

There was a brief silence.

"Okay, we have three big plans in motion," Hugo said. "We'll eliminate Baker and Gibson and get them out of our way for good. We'll destroy a part of the Hidden Empire and let them know we're more powerful than they are. And we'll add a few thousand tons of gold to our fortune."

"Are we still going to wait for the Hidden Empire to start their next meeting in the castle before we launch?" Oleg asked.

"I've decided that's not necessary," Hugo said. "They'll still get the message to not mess with us."

Oleg and Wan raised their right arms into the air. Lucas glanced at them and then made the same gesture.

"We've succeeded in deactivating specific security features at the Federal Reserve Bank of New York and the helicopters should be on their way to pick up the gold," Hugo said.

Wan nodded. "The helicopters should be in New York this afternoon at five o'clock Eastern Standard Time."

Oleg gave a thumbs-up. "And our own state-of-the-art helicopter carrier is sitting out in the Atlantic ready to refuel them on their way here."

Hugo made a circular gesture covering the room. "Okay, I think we have everything working to our satisfaction."

Afterward, someone came to get Lucas to escort him out of the fortress and to the plane. Hugo looked at Wan and said, "On second thought, I think I'll be the one to call Carmen. I want to remind him of something."

Wan nodded.

Hugo reached for his phone.

****

In his luxury mansion in Mexico City, Carmen removed his vibrating phone from under his pillow. With squinted eyes, he looked at the display and could see Hugo was calling.

"I made sure we had a secure connection," Hugo said. "You can talk freely as usual."

"Do you know how early it is over here?" Carmen asked.

"Of course"

"Is this some kind of emergency?"

"In a way," Hugo said. "You and Hector need to leave for Jacksonville in two hours."

"Why?"

"You need to be at our new warehouse in the industrial park to help my assassin, Lucas Becker, kill Baker and Gibson," Hugo said. "And while you're there, you can inspect some things I need you to check."

"What things?" Carmen asked.

"I need you to look around the warehouse and make sure all of your illegal drugs are stored properly," Hugo said. "When possible, you can also look around and check on the missiles that are stored there and the barrels of bio-chemicals."

"We can easily determine if everything is in proper order for the drugs," Carmen said, "but what about the missiles and chemicals? What are we looking for?"

"You need to make sure they're all secured properly and in shielded areas. We don't want the gunfire doing any damage."

"Are we going to have time to do that?"

"If you leave within the next two hours you should get there before your targets arrive."

"Hector and I can get some more expert assassins. Why do we need to do this?"

"Do you have some available right now?"

"We're in the process of getting some more."

"They won't get there in time. You and Hector need to do this. Besides, you owe me after blowing your last assignment with that stupid decision to use the bazooka."

Carmen remained silent.

"Okay, make sure you and Hector are on your way within a couple of hours to be at the warehouse in Jacksonville on time."

"We'll be there on schedule."

"Good, Lucas will meet you at the warehouse and he'll have all the information you need."

Hugo disconnected.

After taking a deep breath and exhaling slowly, he punched in the number for Hector.

****

A few hours later, Lucas Becker, Carmen Vargas, and Hector Medina gathered behind a stack of large wooden crates inside a two-story warehouse in the industrial park in Jacksonville.

They were located on the first floor at the north end of the warehouse, which was about one hundred yards long. Stacks of wooden crates were arranged in a way that provided an aisle the length of the warehouse in the middle and on both sides.

Every ten yards there was an aisle that ran east and west, perpendicular to the main aisles.

Various types of heavy equipment sat on the floor, interrupting the arrangement of the stacks of crates in several places.

"This is the place I selected and it's where Hugo and his team thought I should be," Lucas said. He looked at Carmen and Hector. "They suggested both of you be upstairs but they're leaving that up to us."

Lucas moved out into the middle aisle and gestured toward the south, the front of the warehouse.

Carmen and Hector followed him.

Lucas glanced at the men behind him. "We expect Baker and his group to come in the front entrance." He held his SIG 556 up. "I'll be positioned behind the crates here and prepared to fire. With a 30-round magazine and a 900-shots-per-minute firing rate, I don't think I'll have any trouble getting all of them."

"How often have you had to take down a whole crowd?" Hector asked.

"I've had a lot of sniper assignments," Lucas said. He looked curiously at Hector.

Hector leaned forward. "What's the most you've ever needed to shoot on an assignment?"

Lucas hesitated a moment. "It's been two a few times."

"Has it ever been more than two?" Carmen asked.

Lucas shook his head.

"How did it go when you had to kill two people?" Hector asked.

"I always got both of them but I had to be fast. The second one was always diving for cover."

"Did Hugo tell you how many people we should expect this time?" Carmen asked.

Lucas narrowed his eyes. "He mentioned eight came in their group when they went to the office building. He told me to expect five or six this time."

"They're well experienced in this type of thing. Don't you think it's going to be hard to get more than one of them when you first start shooting?" Hector asked.

Lucas shrugged. "I'm going to give it a try."

Carmen held up his rifle. "We both use an AK-47. It uses 7.62x39 mm ammo in a thirty-round magazine. The rate of fire is 600 rounds per minute but that's never been a problem."

Lucas gave a slow nod. "Hugo told me you both use a Taurus 356 magnum pistol."

Hector nodded. He and Carmen each patted the holster on his right hip.

"So where do you want to be when they come into the building?" Lucas asked.

"Back here with you," Carmen said. "Hector can cover the right aisle and I can cover the left while you cover the middle. I think they're going to scatter quickly when you first start shooting. With three of us covering the area, we'll have a good chance to pick them all off."

"You covering the side aisles from back here is okay with me," Lucas said. "Just wait until I shoot before you open fire."

Carmen and Hector both nodded.

Chapter 26

Later that morning at the Jacksonville FBI Headquarters, Matt, Ralph, Steve, Justin, and Vince sat with Ben in the new control center.

"I think the six of us will be the ideal group to check the warehouse," Ben said. "Hugo has the technology to know what's going on over here and he probably knows we're coming. We'll likely have resistance and I don't think Judy and Todd should be involved in a firefight."

Ralph nodded. "Given the current circumstances, I've made sure they've received some weapons training but they don't have any experience in firefights yet."

Ben punched a button on his control device and several screens on the wall came alive.

Three screens displayed different aerial views of the warehouse. Each view was from a different distance.

Ben punched another button on his control device and one image on a wall-mounted monitor showed three figures entering the front of the warehouse.

In a few more seconds, a close-up of the three figures appeared on one of the screens.

"I'm sure everyone recognizes two of these figures," Ben said.

Justin leaned forward. "It's our old friends Carmen Vargas and Hector Medina. Thought they were in

Mexico."

"They're here now," Ben said. He focused the red dot from his laser pointer on the displayed time.

Matt noted they went into the warehouse an hour ago.

"Who's the other guy?" Steve asked.

Matt narrowed his eyes as he looked at an image of someone who was definitely a warrior.

"He's Lucas Becker," Ben said. "We got the information from RAND. He's obviously going to be in the welcoming committee at the warehouse."

"How did RAND find this out?" Vince asked.

"Some of their analysts just reviewed a ton of new information from NSA, NRO, and some other sources," Ben said. "I'm glad we brought them on board to help review all of our relevant intelligence information and give us their conclusions. I don't know all the details about how they identified him so quickly but they managed to do it."

"Do you have any relevant background information on Lucas Becker?" Ralph asked.

"He's a German sniper who prefers using a SIG 556 rifle and a Heckler & Koch USP pistol," Ben said. "He's known to be one of the better assassins on the planet."

Matt leaned forward. "Looks like we might have a bit more of a challenge than we expected."

"Yep. We're still dealing with one hell of a situation," Ben said, "and we've just received some more information from NSO. They've informed us the group of three is still in the warehouse and they'll inform us immediately if anyone comes outside at any point, especially if they come out on the roof."

"Do you think we should consider using SWAT team apparel and equipment?" Matt asked.

Ben pursed his lips. "Do you have an opinion?"

"Our surveillance resources have been good and it looks like the ambushers are going to stay inside," Matt said. "If that continues to be the case, I feel more comfortable dressing just like we did when we went to the office building before. We certainly did okay then."

Ben glanced at everyone.

They all nodded.

"We handled the two Hispanic assassins well last time and all of our action was outside," Vince said. "Inside we're going to be a lot more restricted as far as getting weapons into the correct firing position quickly but we're probably going to have a lot more cover."

Ben nodded slowly.

"We might each take along a couple of grenades," Ben said. "They could come in real handy in certain situations. I have a good supply of a slimmed-down model that snaps to your belt."

Everyone agreed and Ben soon distributed twelve of them, two each. He also outfitted everyone with tactical microphones and bulletproof vests.

Ben glanced at his watch. "Well, it's about time to mount up. We'll all fit into my SUV. It can hold seven."

Everyone did a last-minute check of the images and data on the screens and then filed out of the room toward the front entrance.

****

Around noon, Ben parked his SUV in the parking lot in front of the same four-story modern office building they had visited before.

The six men got out of the vehicle and cautiously walked in a spread formation toward the large warehouse, which was about 50 yards wide and 100 yards long.

From studying the satellite photos earlier, they had noted there were two large helicopter landing pads on the flat roof.

Matt figured the landing pads were designed for large cargo helicopters that could transport missiles to their launch stations and bio-chemical weapons to their tactical destinations.

As they walked toward the front entrance, each person drew his pistol and kept it in a ready position while staying on full alert.

Ben tried the front door.

It was unlocked.

Ben remained concealed behind the door as he slowly pulled it open.

Nothing happened.

Ben took a step forward and peeped around the door into the warehouse. Everyone else remained on guard and in place along the front wall.

"There's a middle aisle between stacks of wooden crates that runs the length of the warehouse," Ben said into his tactical microphone. "We'll stagger our entrance and rush inside. Get up against the crates on the right of the middle aisle. Stay spread out and we'll form a plan for what we'll do next. I'll go first."

"Roger," everyone replied.

After each person executed as planned and was in position spread horizontally along the first row of crates, Ben said into his tactical microphone, "It looks like there are three aisles. Two of us can go down each aisle toward the back of the warehouse.

"Matt, you and Ralph take the left aisle, Justin and I will take the middle one, and Vince and Steve take the right aisle."

Everyone acknowledged their assignment.

"Okay, let's ease out into position and get started," Ben said.

After checking down the middle aisle carefully, Matt and Ralph rushed across it and stopped close to the end of the row. They maintained a distance of about five yards between them as Matt peered into the left aisle around the corner of the large crate at the end of the row.

Matt estimated the aisle to be about ten yards wide and he cautiously moved into it, staying close to the wooden crates.

Ralph followed about five yards behind.

When Matt got to the first horizontal aisle, he followed the same procedure they had used to cross the middle aisle.

He stopped at the edge of the row of crates and peered to his right down the horizontal aisle. As soon as he determined the aisle was clear he rushed back into the side aisle and to the next horizontal row of crates. He held his Glock 19 straight up with his elbow bent. He kept his finger tight on the trigger.

After about fifty yards, in the middle of the warehouse, Matt and Ralph came to a more open area with some heavy equipment scatted along the concrete floor.

Matt stopped behind a large machine for stacking crates and gestured for Ralph to join him.

Ralph moved up and stopped about a yard away

from Matt.

Both crouched.

"I'm guessing Hugo Wagner has some spy satellites with infrared capability zeroed in on us," Matt whispered.

Ralph nodded. "I don't think there's any doubt about his knowing exactly where all of us are."

"I suggest we stay here for a few minutes. Hugo's probably keeping his people well informed," Matt whispered. "I'll check with everyone on that, okay with you?"

Ralph nodded.

Matt pushed the button to activate his microphone. "Is everyone doing okay?"

Within a few seconds, everyone replied in the affirmative. He let them know about Hugo possibly having infrared capability to zero in on their positions.

"Ralph and I are around the middle of the warehouse and crouched behind some heavy equipment," Matt said. "We're going to stay in place for a while and see if someone comes after us."

"I think Justin and I will do the same thing," Ben replied.

"Ditto," Vince said. "Good luck to all of us."

"Roger that," Matt replied. He reached up and hit the button to turn off his microphone.

Matt looked at Ralph and whispered, "I guess it would be good to try to figure out what someone coming after us might do."

Ralph regarded Matt carefully. "They're probably not going to blow the place up since we know they have missiles and bio-chemical weapons stored here."

"I agree."

Ralph gestured toward the ceiling. "There are a lot of rafters but there's no cover-up there, so they're not going to come that way."

"Agreed, and, speaking of cover, I think we should move up behind the next row of crates," Matt whispered. "That puts us in a better position. We're going to need some good luck no matter what we do."

Ralph nodded. "Our safety factor is about the same whether we're huddled down somewhere or on the move. We have some disadvantages either way."

They moved forward to the next row of crates.

"A lot of skill can overcome a lot of disadvantages," Matt whispered. "Stay alert. We're probably going to get a visitor real soon."

****

Lucas Becker settled into position behind a corner crate on the middle aisle on the back row at the warehouse.

He peered around the corner of the crate and looked toward the front of the warehouse.

Two people suddenly appeared and then darted behind one of the horizontal rows of crates.

Lucas pulled his head fully back behind the crate for a few seconds and then looked out again.

The two figures suddenly appeared, obviously repeating the process they were using.

After remaining hidden behind the crate, Lucas spoke into his tactical microphone, "I have some action. Two people are slowly coming in my direction, ducting in and out of the horizontal rows."

"Nothing over here yet," Carmen said.

Lucas immediately heard Hector's voice. "I have a couple coming my way up the aisle to my right.

They're using the same technique."

Immediately after Hector finished talking, Carmen said, "I now have a couple coming my way too. They're also ducking in and out of the aisles between all the horizontal rows."

"Open fire when they get closer," Lucas said. "It'll be a lot easier to hit them when they're less than twenty yards away."

"Roger," came two replies.

Lucas continued to keep track of the two people who were slowly coming up the main aisle toward him.

All three assassins maintained their position at the back of the warehouse behind a wooden crate on the edge of an aisle.

Lucas again peered down the middle aisle and spotted the two people darting behind the crates on the corner of a horizontal row.

The two people would always wait a few seconds behind each row before they would dart out again and move forward.

Lucas planned to peek around the edge of the crate he was behind and look down the middle aisle about every fifteen seconds.

He was now sure there were only two people in that aisle coming toward him.

The two had been coming for about five minutes.

He had been patient because he figured some more might follow.

But so far, it was just the original two.

He couldn't tell who they were yet—they weren't close enough.

Lucas took in a deep breath, exhaled slowly, and then continued his process. He would wait for them to get within about twenty yards before he fired.

His secure satellite phone vibrated in his pocket. He grabbed it and answered.

"I'm looking at all the infrared images. Are you the one who's standing guard on the middle aisle?" Hugo asked.

"That was the plan, wasn't it?"

"Yes, but I just wanted to be sure you hadn't changed it."

"Two people are coming slowly toward me. They're darting in and out of view."

"I've been watching them."

Lucas took another peek down the aisle. "I can't tell who they are yet. They're not close enough."

"I know who they are and I'm going to get you to change your position."

"How can you tell who they are?"

"We have a profile of their body movements in our quantum computer for each of the six of them. Our computer can run billions of analytical programs within a second."

"Why couldn't you tell who I was?" Lucas asked.

"Because we don't have a profile of body movements for you, Carmen, or Hector stored in our quantum computer," Hugo said. "We didn't think it was necessary since we knew where you were going to be in the warehouse. But in hindsight, it probably would have been a good idea."

Lucas didn't comment.

Hugo gave a short laugh. "However, I solved the problem the old-fashioned way. I just called you and asked where you were."

"Baker and Gibson are over to your right coming

up the left side of the warehouse. Who's over there for us, Carmen or Hector?"

"Hector," Lucas said.

"Notify him you need to trade places. You're our best marksman and Baker and Gibson are our main targets."

"Give me a moment to contact him. I switched my microphone off when I answered your call."

Lucas hit a button and switched his microphone back on.

"Hector, how far away are the people coming toward you?" Lucas asked.

"About sixty yards," Hector said.

"Are they still using the same procedure and coming slowly?"

"Yes."

"Hugo just notified me that the two people coming at you are Baker and Gibson. We're going to switch places. I'm coming your way. Rush over to my position as quickly as you can." Lucas quietly maneuvered forward and passed Hector within a few seconds on his way to his new position.

When Lucas got in place, he immediately spoke into his microphone, "Hector, are you set up?"

"Yes, and the situation is the same as the one I left," Hector said. "I feel like I've been here all along. Two people are still slowly coming my way."

"Carmen, everything still the same with you?" Lucas asked.

"Still the same," Carmen said. "Except for the specific people, we're all dealing with the same situation. And speaking of that, can Hugo tell me who I'm dealing with?"

"Give me a few moments, I'll ask," Lucas said.

After he had conferred with Hugo on the satellite phone, Lucas told Carmen, "Ben Fulton and Justin Mason are coming down the middle aisle. Vince Simmons and Steve Baxter are coming down the side aisle to our left. Both of you already know I'm dealing with Baker and Gibson over here."

"We'll still plan to follow your original advice and wait for you to start firing or for them to get closer."

"Good," Lucas said. "I'll get back in touch if there are any changes."

"Roger," came two replies.

Lucas switched off his tactical microphone and spoke back into his satellite phone. "Any updates?"

"Baker and Gibson are about sixty yards away from you now. You should get ready to take them out pretty soon," Hugo said.

"I want to let them get a little closer?"

"How close?"

"I think letting them get to within about twenty yards will be about right."

"You're an expert marksman. You've shot people from four hundred yards away."

"Those were different circumstances. I was able to get into a stable position and I had a scope on the rifle."

"I think you should let them dart into the next horizontal aisle and then get ready to shoot them as soon as they appear in the aisle again," Hugo said.

"Okay, I'll talk to you later." Lucas disconnected.

Chapter 27

Matt crouched and peeked around the corner of the crate. He pulled back quickly instead of charging out like he usually did.

"What's wrong?" Ralph asked.

"There's a guy down at the end of the warehouse pointing a rifle this way," Matt said.

"Any suggestions?"

"Maybe, but I'm going to take another look first." Matt crouched lower and peeked around the corner again.

The guy with the rifle was still in position.

Matt jerked his head back behind cover. This time, he felt the moving air from the bullets whizzing by. He heard the bullets ricochet off the concrete floor and then crash into something, probably the wall at the front of the warehouse.

"That was close but he wasn't quick enough," Ralph said.

Matt grinned. "Well, we know he's prepared to shoot quickly."

Ralph nodded. "So we definitely don't want to charge him." He took on a more serious expression before he asked, "Think it could be Lucas Becker?"

"That's my guess."

"We know he has the skill to take both of us down before we even cover ten yards, no matter how fast we run in a zigzag pattern."

"Yep, we can't make a frontal assault."

"Think we should move down about ten yards toward the middle aisle in case he comes after us right here?" Ralph said.

Matt stayed in his position and pointed his Glock toward the corner on the side aisle. "That's something to think about but I like my chances better staying put. We'll spread out and stay alert."

Matt started to say more just as a deluge of shots broke out to their right. Some of the shots were closer than others. The firing continued for several seconds.

"Shit!" Ralph said. "That can't be good."

"Yeah, it's unlikely our guys were doing any of the firing. It all sounded like automatic rifle fire."

A brief silence ensued and then there were some more shots.

"Great," Matt said. "Those sounded like pistol shots."

Ralph nodded when more pistol shots rang out. The shots sounded farther away than the other ones.

Everything was quiet again.

"I hope all of our guys are still alive," Matt said.

With their pistols ready and their gazes fixed on the side aisle, they activated their tactical microphones.

"Is anyone there?" Matt asked.

After about a two-second delay, someone answered.

"This is Ben. Justin and I are both okay and Hector Medina is dead."

"What about Vince and Steve?" Ralph asked.

"I was just getting ready to check on them right when you called," Ben said.

"This is Vince. Steve and I are both okay and Carmen Vargas is also dead."

"Great!" Their words blended together seamlessly as Matt and Ralph spoke in perfect unison.

"I heard some gunfire over on your side," Ben said. "Are you both okay?"

"Yeah, we're okay," Matt replied. "Lucas was firing down the aisle. He's at the corner of the last row of crates at the back of the warehouse. You might hear some more in just a moment. I'm going to take another look."

Matt looked at Ralph and gestured back toward the side aisle.

Both men moved back to the corner and stayed alert, pistols pointed toward the aisle.

Matt crouched even lower. His head was almost on the floor when he peeked around the corner again.

Lucas was still in the same position and he fired multiple times in rapid succession.

Matt, fully prepared, jerked back behind cover. Once more, he again felt the rush of air as the bullets whizzed by him. The bullets ricocheted off the concrete floor right at the corner of the wooden crate and then crashed into something, probably another wooden crate this time. It sounded like wood splintering.

Lucas had obviously aimed right where Matt's head had been.

"Well, he's still in position—any new ideas on how to flush him out?" Ralph asked.

Matt activated his tactical microphone. "Ben, can you or one of the others go after Lucas from the side?"

"I'm in the process of doing that. I'm almost to the back row," Ben said. "I'll stop at the corner and peek around the crate on that side of the middle aisle to see if I have a view of Lucas. If I do, I'll start shooting at him."

"That should work," Matt replied. "Lucas is probably still concentrating on getting me, so that might distract him."

"Roger," Ben said. "Vince, you and Steve leave this up to me. I don't want one of you to shoot me when I step out into the back aisle."

"Roger," Vince replied.

In less than a minute, Ben reported that he was in position and could see Lucas down at the end of the row.

Matt heard a barrage of pistol shots coming from the vicinity of the middle aisle at the back of the warehouse. He peered around the corner of the crate he was behind.

Lucas staggered out in the side aisle and tried to turn toward the middle of the warehouse. Matt realized the man was wearing bullet-proof clothing.

Carefully, Matt stepped fully out into the aisle, extended his pistol and aimed at Lucas' head.

As Matt's finger pulled the trigger, Lucas jerked around in shock, his eyes widening with disbelief before crumpling to the ground with a loud thud.

"We got him," Matt informed his team.

Within a minute, the group of six huddled in the back aisle.

They all stayed alert for any surprises as Justin removed his phone from a pocket and made a call.

A short while later, about twenty policemen flooded the area. Three carried body bags.

Some in tactical outfits checked the upstairs.

Everything was clear.

After Justin and Vince had short conversations with some of the policemen, Ben waved everyone in his group toward the front entrance.

"I'll get a team over here to inspect the missiles and bio-chemical weapons upstairs," Ben said.

Matt felt relieved they had finished this part but there was a lot of work left on the overall situation.

"We'll go back to the FBI building," Ben said. "We have to determine our plan of action to take next."

****

Hugo slammed his right fist on the rounded desktop in front of him. "Damned, Baker and his group survived another attack."

Oleg and Wan remained silent.

"Nothing has gone right." Hugo scowled. "With the technology at our disposal, we should be able to do whatever we want to do, but we keep failing." Hugo pressed his lips together tightly and shook his head. He exhaled sharply and then looked at Wan. "We have a lot of other things to deal with too. When are your scientists going to figure out what happened with our trying to shut down the security system at the Federal Reserve Bank of New York?"

"They've concluded the Feds have a quantum computer defending their system," Wan said. "We know some professors developed one at the University of Florida and it's likely they're applying it at the Federal Reserve System. We're in the process of collecting more data about that."

"I pulled the helicopters back and now, with Carmen and Hector gone, we need to get someone else to manage them." Hugo looked directly at Wan. "Do you think your scientists can resolve the hacking problem in the Federal Reserve System anytime soon?"

"My scientists have set up a test system with two quantum computers," Wan said. "One computer will try to break into the system the other quantum computer controls. They're collecting a lot of additional data that should help them but I don't know how soon they can resolve this problem."

Hugo nodded slowly and then picked up his vibrating phone. He listened for a moment and looked at Oleg and Wan. "We have some issues with preparing the missiles. You're both involved in getting them ready to fire. I need to know how much longer that's going to take."

Oleg glanced at Wan. "Your Chinese scientists are much more involved in all the details than my scientists. You can check things and give him an answer."

"Yeah, but they're Russian missiles," Wan said. "Your scientists are much more familiar with the basic technology."

Oleg furrowed his brow. "The missiles have a lot of modifications your scientists made to improve them."

"Someone give me a damned answer. We've just had a serious setback and I need to make some decisions on what actions to take next," Hugo said.

Wan leaned forward. "Oleg and I will go together over to the missile site and check on things." He looked at Hugo. "We'll get you a reliable answer as soon as possible."

"Make it fast," Hugo said. "We need to send a strong message to the Hidden Empire."

A flashing red light on one of the displays immediately caught everyone's attention.

"Someone has launched missiles at us," Wan said. "Two missiles were detected, and our defense system has already launched interceptors."

The display showed one incoming missile had already been destroyed.

"We have the best defense system in the world," Hugo said. "It's impossible for…"

Chapter 28

The next morning in Florida, the team sat with Ben at the large table in the main conference room in the Jacksonville FBI Headquarters.

"Well, we got the job done at the warehouse and we eliminated three more of the assassins Hugo Wagner sent to kill us," Ben said. "Luckily, Justin had just jumped behind a corner crate when Hector started firing."

Vince nodded. "Steve and I did something similar going after Carmen, but we were a little more limited on what we could do being on a side aisle." He gestured to Steve.

"Yeah, we only had one side of the aisle where we could make use of the wooden crates," Steve said. "I went first while Vince stayed behind a corner crate and kept his pistol in position to fire toward the corner of the last row of crates. I ran toward the back of the warehouse and ducked behind cover when I got to each row of crates."

"Did you have a plan if Carmen started firing when you were in between rows?" Matt asked.

Steve gave a short laugh. "Yeah, dive to the floor and hope that Vince could get him quickly."

"And I did," Vince said.

Ralph and Matt grinned.

"That certainly opened up the opportunity to get

Lucas Becker," Matt said, "and we took advantage of it."

Ben started to comment when his phone beeped, signaling he had received a message.

After Ben read the message, he said, "I've received a lot of new information from all of our intelligence agencies. NSA has intercepted a lot of calls and NRO has sent new images."

The room fell into a hushed silence, waiting for Ben to continue.

"We have a lot more to talk about than just what's been going on here." Ben scanned the faces around the table. "It looks like Hugo Wagner and his operation has been wiped off the face of the earth."

"What happened?" Matt asked.

"Sources in Germany reported there was a nuclear explosion in the mountains in the southern part of the country," Ben said. "We'll get into the details in a few moments but the bottom line is that it looks like the target was Hugo Wagner and his operation."

Justin narrowed his eyes. "I thought Hugo was in the northern part of Germany."

"That's what we thought but it looks like he was actually in the southern part," Ben said. "We all know he was an expert at deception." He started to say more when his phone vibrated on the table.

Ben checked the caller-ID and answered.

After a short discussion, Ben disconnected and looked at everyone.

"The CIA and the German Government have jointly confirmed that Hugo Wagner and his hidden fortress in Germany have been completely destroyed by a tactical nuclear missile," Ben said. "They suspect it was a Russian missile and they're in the process of confirming that."

"Does anyone know if it was the Hidden Empire who made the strike?" Ralph asked.

"I know all of our intelligence agencies have been trying to determine if the Russians, the KGB in particular, are masterminding everything or if other elements of the Hidden Empire are," Ben said. "There's a lot we don't know about all this."

Judy gave a short laugh. "Yeah, and we don't even know how much we don't know."

Ben narrowed his eyes and looked at Judy. "Have you found any new relevant financial information about what we're dealing with?"

"Todd and I have been in the process of connecting a lot of dots on the financial arrangement Hugo had set up," Judy said. "We think China has been controlling a lot of the financial aspects recently. Wan Lu was the main connection between Hugo Wagner and China on that."

"The increased Chinese involvement in all the various things we're involved with is disturbing," Ben said. "But if some Chinese groups are actually part of the Illuminati that would make sense."

Todd nodded. "Judy and I have completed a lot of research on many aspects of the Hidden Empire. It's definitely global and it looks like a lot of countries are part of it. We're still trying to get the specifics."

"All of the members are loyal only to their organization. They have little or no loyalty to their countries," Judy said.

Ben pressed his lips together and leaned forward. "So that's why they'll go against their own countrymen when it's necessary to keep their organization from receiving a setback."

"That has jumped out to Todd and me during our research," Judy said. "The existence of the Federal Reserve System and its unimpeded operation apparently is essential to the funding for the Hidden Empire. Anything that threatens that has to be eliminated."

Todd nodded. "That's why the members of the Hidden Empire at the time took drastic measures to make sure the Federal Reserve was created."

"And a few years after the Federal Reserve was formed in 1913, the International Acceptance Bank of New York was created in 1921 to grease the wheels of the money flow so to speak," Judy said. "The World Bank, WTO, IMF, and other components of the global money flow were added later to fine-tune the overall financial system."

"Before the Federal Reserve System was created the United States went through a financial panic back in 1907 didn't it?" Matt asked.

"Yes," Judy said. "A lot of banks failed and that adversely affected everyone, including millionaires."

Todd grunted. "Yeah, and the adverse effects went on for a few years. President Theodore Roosevelt had signed a bill creating the National Monetary Commission in 1908 and that helped to some extent but a bunch of the most powerful millionaires in New York and some government officials banded together and decided to do something to keep the panic from happening again."

A brief silence ensued.

"Without getting into all the nitty-gritty details about how they all profited from setting up the system,

I'll just simply point out it worked for them and they're very serious about keeping it working for them," Judy said. "There are a lot of powerful people out there who get very upset when they find out someone is going to do some damage to how it works."

"It obviously didn't work well for the general population back then since we had the great depression that started in 1929."

"Like I mentioned, it worked for the millionaires," Judy said. "And the descendants of the original group plan to keep it working for them. They certainly will take drastic action against anyone who poses a serious threat to the continued existence of the system."

Ben shook his head slowly. "The bottom line here is simple to understand, but clearly understanding all the ramifications of how things are set up and exactly how they work is off the charts."

Todd gave a short laugh. "Yeah, it's the most complicated puzzle Judy and I have ever seen. The trails lead all over the place but I think we've put many of the pieces together rather well so far and we'll continue to work on it."

Ben looked at Todd and Judy. "You're a big help. We certainly know a lot more about global funding and how various aspects of that apply to almost everything we're contending with."

"Now that Hugo Wagner is out of the picture I guess we need to pay more attention to the Hidden Empire as we move forward with our hopefully more normal activities," Matt said.

Ben narrowed his eyes. "As long as we don't do something that threatens the Hidden Empire we should be able to return to normal."

Matt realized they had a long way to go before they resolved a lot of mysteries they might have to deal with as they moved forward with Tuxtun's global business.

Chapter 29

The next morning in Western Europe, about twenty miles east of Zurich, Vulcan, Neptune, and Apollo gathered in their usual place in the ancient elaborate castle.

"I thought just the three of us needed to get back together and sort through things," Vulcan said. "Don't know about you, but I still have an unsettled feeling. We also have a new agenda to review and we need to give our joint opinion about some things. There are several significant new decisions we need to make."

Per their usual routine, Vulcan and Neptune each filled their pipes with their favorite tobacco and took a long puff.

Apollo waited patiently for Vulcan to start the discussion.

"Well, we've completely eliminated Hugo Wagner and his organization. I learned that Thor was in charge of all the details for the missile strike and he executed perfectly," Vulcan said. "Hugo Wagner and his entire organization will no longer pose a threat to us."

"So our global money flow will remain as usual?" Apollo asked.

Vulcan gave a slight shrug. "I think some adjustments will need to be made as we go forward with all the AI stuff becoming more prevalent. That's on our list of items to be discussed in the near future. It isn't easy to keep everything tuned properly when it's so complex."

"Why does it need to be as complex as it is?" Apollo asked.

"None of the payments we make to various important people around the world must ever be traced," Vulcan said. "We have to constantly make payments to the right influential leaders to ensure important events go the way we need them to."

"Hugo had established a very secure fortress and he had the second-best technology on the planet." Neptune took a long puff from his pipe and leaned forward. "It was a remarkable feat we were able to stop him."

"I guess we're the ones who have the best technology on the planet, right?" Apollo asked.

Neptune and Vulcan chuckled briefly before inhaling deeply on their pipes.

Apollo shrugged. "That wasn't a stupid question. I just wanted to make sure I completely understood what you were saying. It never hurts to clarify things to make sure there are no misunderstandings."

"You have a good point," Vulcan said. "We're currently well embedded in every major country around the globe and we intend to stay that way. That's how we'll eventually reach our goal of a one-world government."

Neptune and Apollo gave a thumbs-up.

"It's great to be able to come back here," Vulcan said.

Apollo looked at Vulcan. "But we know the group at Tuxtun is continuing to try to analyze it. Do you think that could turn out to be a problem for us?"

"I asked Zeus about that and he told me he had discussed it with Jupiter and Odin," Vulcan said. "They're going to watch that activity closely and take any necessary action. Right now they don't think there'll be a problem if Tuxtun doesn't try to interfere with something critical to our money flow."

Apollo and Neptune both nodded.

"Zeus also told me our financial group has made some recent enhancements to the procedures and activities of the World Trade Organization over in Geneva and to the Bank for International Settlements over in Basel," Vulcan said. "After some additional close analysis on how our global money flow is working, our group of financial experts decided to make some adjustments to keep the details even more hidden."

"Did Zeus give you any specifics?" Apollo asked.

"He did give me some more information. He mentioned our financial experts were also looking into making some adjustments to the procedures and activities of the Federal Open Market Committee and the Institute of International Finance."

"I'm not familiar with them. What do they do?" Apollo asked.

"They mainly just fill in some gaps in our global money flow," Vulcan said. He smiled and then took a long, slow puff on his pipe. "Like I mentioned earlier, we'll discuss some of that in future meetings if we need to."

A brief silence ensued.

Neptune grunted. "Well, I'm glad the three of us can get back to our normal operations."

"I know some financial analysts in the intelligence

agencies are still working to fully define the global financial system. The group at Tuxtun is still working with them," Apollo said. "I guess they want to understand the mechanics of how it all works for some reason."

Vulcan leaned forward. "Don't worry. They'll never figure it out. Zeus assured me of that."

"But that analytical activity could turn out to be a problem for us in the long run, don't you think?" Apollo asked.

"If it does, our leaders won't allow it to continue," Vulcan said.

Apollo looked unconvinced.

"Zeus told me our financial analysts are keeping a close eye on what the combined intelligence agencies/Tuxtun group is doing but our analysts don't think that group will ever be able to figure it out," Vulcan said. "It's so complex that even our financial experts have to go back to the original blueprint and then review a lot of the changes we've made over the years to understand things properly."

Apollo regarded Vulcan carefully. "Did you by any chance mention my concern directly to Zeus?"

"Yes I did and that's when he told me our financial experts are watching them closely," Vulcan said. "But again, he's not worried right now about our having any problems resulting from their analysis."

Apollo narrowed his eyes. "But that whole group includes a lot of very capable and very smart people. If they're given enough time I think they'll figure out at least some of the critical details of our system, certainly enough to give us some problems."

"Remember, we're keeping a close eye on them,"

Vulcan said. "And even if they do figure some things out, I don't think they would feel the need to take any action."

Neptune grunted. "And even if that group did feel the need to take some action I don't think they would be able to change anything."

"That's right," Vulcan said. "We're in complete control. We have people in position to make changes when we need them and they're the only people who can make the changes."

"Hugo was able to get some of his people in position to allow him to use parts of our system," Apollo said.

Vulcan took a long puff on his pipe and looked at Apollo. "Yeah, but remember he could only use parts of our system. That's why he had to create all the shell companies."

"And also Hugo's people couldn't make any changes in our system. They were very limited on what they could do." Neptune took a long slow puff on his pipe. "I think we can relax on that subject and concentrate on other things we need to discuss."

"That's correct," Vulcan said. "Our leaders will keep up with what's going on and I'm sure they'll take any necessary action they need to."

Chapter 30

The next morning in Jacksonville, the team met with Ben in the new hi-tech control room in the Jacksonville FBI Headquarters.

Ben focused the red dot from his laser pointer on one of the large screens on the wall. The image on the screen was obviously shown from a high altitude. It showed a green forest in a mountainous area. The red dot on the screen rested over a huge depression in the middle of the area.

"This gigantic hole in the ground is where Hugo Wagner's fortress complex was about twenty-four hours ago," Ben said. "Obviously, his location wasn't as hidden as he thought it was."

Matt nodded. "And his technology wasn't as dominant either."

"And that's a rather sobering thought," Ben said. He looked at everyone. "Hopefully, we won't have any more threats from any remaining parts of what he set up," Ben said. "But the Hidden Empire is obviously still out there. I hope nothing we're doing poses a threat to them. We certainly don't want to continue dealing with them or their assassins."

Matt narrowed his eyes as his gaze took in Todd and Judy. "Have you come up with anything new on the Hidden Empire?"

"Not really. The problem is when you try to nail

down all the specifics about them, the trails run into infinity," Judy said. "Todd and I are still working with financial analysts at RAND and all the intelligence agencies but the Hidden Empire is an entirely different animal than Hugo Wagner's organization was."

Todd leaned forward. "And for them to have wiped out Hugo's organization off the map, the Hidden Empire have proven they have the best technology on the planet."

Everyone agreed.

"It wasn't so difficult to stay hidden for centuries, but in modern times you would think they would need the best technology to help provide sufficient cover for all their activities."

"Once we have a chance to catch our breath at Tuxtun we'll decide on whether or not we move forward immediately with our global business plans," Ralph said. "There's a good chance we'll wait a while. It's probably smart to let things stabilize a bit more before we jump back into our more ambitious plans. We'll continue to work closely with the CIA to keep up with what's going on in Mexico and South America."

"Todd and I have been reviewing a lot of the information we've already collected," Judy said. "We know the drug cartels will continue to use the schemes Hugo Wagner set up for them to support their global money flow. We'll need to completely unravel that maze."

"And we know the Hidden Empire uses a lot of similar schemes," Todd said. "However, they don't need to set up shell companies. They have a huge structure already set up for them."

Judy leaned forward. "They have a legal global

network that can hide a huge amount of activity from public view."

Steve grunted. "The more we know about the global monetary system the easier it will be to discover all of the drug cartels methods for laundering money and maybe cut off some of their funding."

"We had better be prepared if the cartels come after us." Matt looked at Steve.

Steve rubbed his chin. "We've already improved our security system here at work, including establishing a secure parking lot for us and all of our employees. Also, we've all improved our home security so we should be in good shape if we end up coping with more threats."

Ralph nodded.

"I think we're well prepared at the moment to cope with more threats," Steve said. "I'll continue to study the situation and recommend any needed adjustments to our security."

Ben looked at Ralph. "And you'll probably need to be real careful on a lot of fronts as you move forward on expanding your business. And speaking of expanding your business…Tuxtun already makes some legal drugs like morphine and codeine, right?"

"That's right, and we want to expand our production," Ralph said. "That's why we need more crops of poppies. That's our starting point for being able to produce the morphine and codeine."

"Those last two drugs you mentioned are made from poppy straw, aren't they?" Justin asked.

"Concentrate of poppy straw," Ralph said. "It's referred to as CPS and it's every bit legal, all going to American pharmaceutical companies."

"Well, I guess my point is that you'll be competing with the drug cartels on growing the poppies and producing the CPS." Ben gave a slight shrug. "Some might get irritated about some things and try to knock you off."

Ralph grunted. "Yeah, Matt and I have talked about that." He made a sweeping gesture. "Thanks to all the support from law enforcement we're well trained in every aspect of defending ourselves."

"And we now have a lot more experience dealing with trained assassins," Matt said. "I think we're in good shape to deal with any new threats."

Ralph nodded. "And we don't have Hugo Wagner and his organization to deal with anymore. That simplifies everything quite a bit."

"But you still have the Hidden Empire out there and the chance you might step on their toes as you continue to analyze the global monetary flow," Ben said. "And judging by what they did to Hugo, they can almost certainly eliminate you if they choose to do so."

Matt turned toward Ben. "I think you're right but Hugo was getting ready to interfere with their operations, we're not. And we'll try to be real careful we don't interfere with any of their operations as we go forward. That's a big reason to keep learning more about the global monetary system."

"That might be hard to do since none of us even know what their operations are," Ben said.

Matt gestured toward Judy and Todd. "They'll be our eyes and ears, and we know a lot more now than we used to. We'll remain vigilant and exercise caution with our current operations and expand our future growth."

****

With Hugo and his organization annihilated, the Hidden Empire now settled back, satisfied, operating in familiar territory: continuing their normal activity.

Leaders of this powerful shadow group were again confident they could handle any future threats.

A word about the author...

Thomas Velsun lives with his wife in coastal Florida. He's a former Army officer and a veteran of the Viet Nam War. After leaving the Military he spent over thirty years in business and is retired from a large global technology company.

During his business career, he completed special projects with various government agencies in Washington DC, including the FBI, CIA, US Mint, and IRS. He has participated in special projects with RAND Corporation (a think tank formed after World War II to continue the activities of various experts accumulated during the war years). He has worked in many different areas in the United States and in foreign countries. He has researched many conspiracy theories and has included selected subject matter from some of them in his novels.

He's a former athlete and maintains fitness with daily workouts involving weightlifting. He also enjoys playing golf and tennis.